DANNY ORLIS
AND HIS CRISES AT
CEDARTON

DANNY ORLIS AND HIS CRISES AT CEDARTON

BERNARD PALMER

Danny Orlis and His Crises at Cedarton
© 2024 by Bernard Palmer
All rights reserved. First edition 1971.
Second edition 2024.

Please do not reproduce, store in a retrieval system, or transmit in any form or by any means – electronic, mechanical, photocopying, recording, or otherwise, without written permission from the publisher.

Scripture quotations from The Authorized (King James) Version. Rights in the Authorized Version in the United Kingdom are vested in the Crown. Reproduced by permission of the Crown's patentee, Cambridge University Press.

Cover image: Adobe Firefly
Character illustrations: John Ball
Editor: Charlene Miskimen

Aneko Press Youth

www.anekopress.com

Aneko Press, Life Sentence Publishing, and our logos are trademarks of Life Sentence Publishing, Inc.
203 E. Birch Street
P.O. Box 652
Abbotsford, WI 54405

JUVENILE FICTION / Religious / Christian / Action & Adventure

Paperback ISBN: 978-1-62245-986-5

eBook ISBN: 978-1-62245-987-2

10 9 8 7 6 5 4 3 2 1

Available where books are sold

CONTENTS

CHAPTER 1

A DIFFICULT DECISION

The Northwest Angle of the Lake of the Woods was lying glassy-calm that evening, shimmering like so many acres of polished marble in the dying sun. The hush of autumn laid its benediction on muskeg and water alike, marred only by the discordant snarl of Danny Orlis's outboard motor.

As he neared the place where he was going to fish, just beyond the mouth of Harrison Creek, he cut the throttle to idling speed and moved cautiously toward the patch of reeds with the stealth of a hunter stalking moose. Once within casting range he flicked off his outboard motor and let the small boat glide to a halt. The water was so motionless he didn't even need the anchor that lay at his feet.

Briefly he listened to the slap of his wake against the rocks. Only when the spreading row of waves stopped their loud talking and began to whisper did he turn his attention to the purpose of his evening excursion on the lake.

He picked up his spinning rod and flicked the red and white metal wobbler to the edge of the rushes. The instant the lure slapped the surface a large northern pike lunged at it, coming out of the water in a mighty surge of power. Danny's rod arced, and line squealed from the reel.

A grin chased the frown lines from his bronzed face. He didn't know why, but he always thrilled at the determined rush of a hooked fish, at matching his skill against the muscular force of a worthy adversary. And when he had boated them, he would just as soon turn them loose. When he had caught a couple of fish for the table, the rest went back.

He hadn't had much of an opportunity to fish lately. There had been a steady stream of customers at his dad's little fishing camp and he had been guiding most of the time. Now, however, school was about to start once more and the fishermen had tapered off. Only that morning the last party of tourists had gone out on the *Island Queen,* and for the first time in weeks, the Orlis family was alone at Angle Inlet.

Danny brought the fish to the boat, netted it and removed the hook, pausing long enough to watch the graceful flight of a blue heron on its way to the opposite shore for the night.

Usually he enjoyed this time of year more than any other. It was a quiet, leisurely time, for one thing.

The fishing season was over and the hunting had not yet begun. The winter's wood was already sawed and split and piled close to the back door. The boats had to be gone over, the rental motors prepared for winter, and guides for the hunting season secured, but it was a time of late breakfasts and lingering over coffee at lunch and dinner. It was a time for canning wild blueberries and cranberries, a time of enjoying the last brief days of summer.

This year was the same as any other for the rest of the family, but Danny had no rest. His parents and Kay Milburn and just about everyone else he knew expected him to go away to Bible school again. He had a letter from Kay in his pocket that had come only that afternoon. Even though he had been hinting in his letters to her that he might not be back at Cedarton Bible Institute that fall, she kept right on assuming that he would be there.

"I suppose you are as anxious to get back to CBI as I am," she had written. "I think I'm going to be leaving home a week early this year. When do you think you'll be coming?"

That simple question set him aflame. When would he be coming? When indeed?

It made him furious just to think about it! Why did she have to be so sure that he was coming back to CBI when he didn't know himself?

And his mom and dad were the same as Kay. The last week or two all they had been able to talk about was his going to Bible school again. But, come to think of it, that was the way they had been ever since he could remember. Even before he had gone away to high school, they had been talking about his going to Bible school. As far as they were concerned, it was all settled. That was one of the things that made it so hard for him. They would both be terribly hurt if he didn't go back to CBI. They wouldn't even consider the fact that they needed him at home.

And they did need him. Danny knew that without asking. They had needed him that summer during the fishing season. There were any number of tourists who stayed because they were able to get a guide who knew the lake and could get them to where the fish were. And there was always heavy work that his dad shouldn't be doing alone.

It was even more important that he be there during the hunting season. Mom and Dad wouldn't have Ron's help then and the work was even heavier. He didn't know why it was, but hunters half his dad's age would allow him to do all the hard work simply because they were paying him. Danny had seen his dad come in after a day of hunting, his face ashen with fatigue. He had heard his mother say that there were times when his dad couldn't sleep, he was so exhausted. Yet he had to be up before dawn the next day, doing the same thing over again.

Danny Orlis cast again, but his mind was not on his fishing. As far as he was concerned, there was no doubt about it. His dad and mom needed him at home, and he had to do something about it. He didn't care how much they protested.

He had reached that conclusion slowly, and not without a certain amount of difficulty. After all, there had been that time, just before school ended the spring before, when he renewed his decision to turn his life completely over to God. He didn't want to go back on that, either.

Kay's attitude toward the decision she had made at the same time disturbed him most, he reasoned. As far as she was concerned, deciding to give God complete control of her life was only another big step along the road to the mission field. She hadn't told Danny he should do the same thing, but her decision had influenced him. He began to feel led to the mission field himself, urged on, no doubt, by Kay's excitement when he told her what he had been considering.

At that time he hadn't really stopped to weigh the cost. It would take him away from the Northwest Angle that he loved so much.

Danny paused, motionless, while a moose came down to the lakeshore some distance away. The stately animal moved majestically out of the bush, pausing at the water's edge and looking about, his massive head and rack held high. Then, satisfied that there was no danger lurking nearby, he stepped proudly into the water and began to feed on the weeds and lily pads around him. Danny watched, awe holding him motionless. He didn't know how many times he had viewed that same scene but it still thrilled him. It was small wonder that he began to ache inside when he thought about leaving the Angle.

When Danny finally got back to the house that evening, his dad was sitting in the living room, a magazine open on his lap. Carl Orlis looked up and greeted him. Presently he asked the question Danny knew he would ask.

"What did Kay have to say?"

Danny shrugged. "I guess she's going to CBI a week or so early this fall for some reason."

"What does that mean?" Carl asked, laughter in his voice. "Are we going to lose you a week early, too?"

He squirmed uncomfortably. "That's what I want to talk to you about, Dad."

His dad misunderstood him. "We don't have any fishermen coming between now and Labor Day that I know of. And if we should get a little business, I think Mom and I can manage all right. If you want to go to school early, there's no reason why it can't be arranged."

Danny's face clouded. He had been afraid the conversation would go that way.

"That isn't really what I want to talk with you about, Dad," he began, fumbling for words. "It looks to me as though you're going to have a big hunting season. Maybe the biggest you've had for several years."

"We can thank God for that."

"But it's going to make an awful lot of work for you. That's what concerns me."

"The only real problem we're going to have is in getting guides. We're going to get some of our old guides back, but we always lose a few." He inhaled deeply. "I was just thinking about that tonight. I ought to go over to the reserve tomorrow and see if I can get a few more."

Hiring guides was a problem, Danny knew. The hunting was done on the Canadian side of the Lake of the Woods and had to be done according to Ontario regulations, which called for a resident guide for each two hunters. But getting guides wasn't the sort of work Danny was concerned about. His dad could do that without any trouble.

It was the physical labor that concerned Danny, the back-breaking work that was a part of every hunting trip. His dad didn't move as fast as he used to, and he got tired more easily. He shouldn't be working as hard as he had been.

"Dad," Danny began suddenly, "what would you think if I told you that I'd like to stay home from school this year and help you?"

He didn't know what he expected his dad to do, but he was surprised that his expression did not change.

"I'm sure you mean well, Danny, but Mom and I can't ask you to make a sacrifice like that." His smile was calm and reassuring. "We may complain a little, but actually, we can get along fine. You don't have to worry about us. We've been taking care of ourselves for quite a number of years, you know."

"That's just it!" Danny retorted with feeling. "You shouldn't be working as hard as you do. If I stayed home this year I could take over a lot of the work you do, Dad. You wouldn't have to work so hard during the hunting season."

Carl Orlis rolled his magazine tightly. "I know how you feel, but that would be against our wishes, Danny. It would be against everything we've ever wanted for you – against anything we've ever prayed for you."

"You can't go on this way, Dad. You've got to have help." He paused. "I'm not going to be turning my back on the Lord. I'm going to keep on living for Him."

"I'm sure you would."

"You seem to forget that I can do a lot of work for the Lord right here on the Angle. There are a lot of our neighbors here who need spiritual help. I can talk with them about their need for a Savior."

"I suppose you could, Danny," Carl Orlis said.

What Danny said was true, Carl had to admit. And, humanly speaking, he would be most happy to have Danny stay at home with them for a year, or even all the time, for that matter. They could certainly use him. He and Mary were both tired–very tired. The lines were deepening in her face, and he knew the extra work of the hunting and fishing seasons was hard for her. It was harder for him to keep things up the way they should be. A little chore like mowing the grass had become a real burden the last couple of years. And scooping snow and cutting the firewood were both harder for him to do than he would ever let anyone know.

It would be good to have Danny around to take the harder work of the hunting season for him. But he wasn't willing to pay the price for that help that he would have to pay.

"Maybe this is exactly what God wants me to do," Danny continued.

Carl's gaze found his. "Perhaps it is, son, but I have the feeling that you wouldn't have to work so hard to convince yourself of it if it actually is God's will."

The boy winced. "I've spent a lot of time thinking about this, Dad. I'm almost convinced that it's what I should do this year. Maybe I could stay home for one semester, just to help you with the hunting season."

"I'm not going to tell you what to do, Danny. You're too old for that. Besides, I'd just be getting in the way. This is something between you and God. You've got to decide, first of all, whether staying home or going to Bible school this year is God's will for you. After you make that decision, you've got to decide whether you're going to follow Him or whether you're going to make your own plans. The only other thing I'm going to say is that you aren't going to be happy until you are in God's particular place for you, whatever that place may be."

Danny eyed him irritably. If his dad had been argumentative, he could have given him argument for argument, as persuasive and logical as he gave out. Danny had already gone through all of those things in his mind. He was prepared to argue. But his dad hadn't argued. He had thrown the ball back to him. He was going to have to answer it himself.

Danny brushed his hand across his face. He didn't know what was the matter with his dad. Why didn't he help him make up his mind about whether to go back to school or not?

CHAPTER 2

AN UNWANTED ANSWER

The next few days Danny's mind was awash with emotion. One minute he was sure that he should stay at the Angle and help his dad, at least through the first semester. It was definitely what God would have him do. The next minute, he wondered if he shouldn't go back to school. He knew how hard it would be to break away from the Angle again and continue his studies after being out for a time. He had heard guys talk about dropping out of school to pay for a car or some bad debts and that they never did go back and finish. If God had led him to CBI in the first place, why would He lead him back to the Angle? Did God change His mind?

Danny supposed he was glad that his dad and mom were leaving the decision up to him, but he would have appreciated their guidance. Not that he needed it to know what they wanted him to do. There had never been any doubt about that. They would be greatly disturbed if he stayed home with them, as badly as they needed him.

The closest his mother had come in attempting to influence him had been to ask him if he had made up his mind or not. When he told her he hadn't, she didn't press the matter but mumbled something about wanting to get his clothes ready if he was going.

And there was always Kay. He had only hinted to her that he might not be coming back. He hadn't told her outright that he didn't think he would be back. If he had, she would not try to get him to change his mind. She was like that. But it was obvious from her letters that she expected him to come back for his second year.

Then a letter came from the school president, a brief, friendly letter that said he hoped to see Danny back at CBI when school opened in September. That was all he wrote, but it affected the boy strangely. If Dr. Norton would take the time to write to him inviting him back to school, perhaps he ought to reconsider. Perhaps this was God's way of letting him know His will. He would go, he decided, and see if he could get a job that would pay his expenses, or most of them.

"I've decided to go to CBI and give it a whirl," he told his parents, "but I'm not going to be a burden to you. If I can get a job, I'll take that to mean that God wants me there. If I don't, I'll assume He was just testing me to see if I would go and that He really wants me here helping you."

Relief gleamed in his parents' eyes. "We're so thankful for that. You'll never know how we've been praying that you'd go back to school."

He bristled slightly as he saw how pleased they were. "But remember, no job, no school. I'm not going there and cost you a lot of money that you have to work so hard to get."

"You worked here all summer for spending money, Danny," Carl Orlis said. "I've been planning to pay you for your tuition and your board and room."

"Not this year!" Danny broke in roughly. "I've taken help from you long enough. This year I'm going to make it on my own or I'm going to come back here and work. I've put out the fleece the way Gideon did. If God wants me there, He'll provide me with a job that's good enough to make it possible for me to earn my own way."

His mother eyed him reproachfully but only said, "We'll be praying for you, Danny."

He fell silent, suddenly rebuked. But others had done the same thing, he told himself defensively. He had talked with any number of kids at CBI who trusted God for their needs. And if the money didn't come, they took that as a sign that God didn't want them to have what they had been praying for, even to the point of going to school or not going. What was so bad about his praying the same way?

Danny had waited so long to make up his mind about going back to school that he had to scurry to get things ready in the few days remaining. His mother had gotten some of his clothes ready ahead of time, however, in hope that he would make up his mind to return to CBI, and it wasn't long until everything was packed. He left the Angle on the *Island Queen* for Warroad where he caught a bus to Cedarton.

There were two other CBI students on the bus, guys he had known briefly the year before. Both of them were excited about getting back to school and could talk of little else.

"I thought I was going to get to school early," one of them said, "so I could have a better chance of getting a good job. But I couldn't make it. I was helping with Bible camp and we just finished last week. So I guess I'll be pushing a broom again this year, the same as last."

"Not me," his companion put in. "I worked on construction all summer so I've got a little money saved. I don't want to have to work such long hours this year in order to stay in school. I think my grades suffered from it."

Danny entered into the conversation at intervals, but he really wasn't listening to what was being said. His mind alternated between Angle Inlet where his dad was making final preparations for the hunting season and the school where everybody but him thought he ought to go.

And he still didn't know for sure how he felt about it. In one way he would like to get a job so he could stay at Cedarton. In another, he was anxious to get back home and help his parents.

When he got to the dorm he learned that Kay had arrived at CBI several days before and had been asking about him.

"I didn't know you were so popular with her, Danny," his roommate said. "Every time the phone rings it's Kay wanting to know whether you're here yet or not."

"Come off it, John," Danny said laughing. "You're putting me on."

"You just wait. In less than twenty minutes the phone'll ring and a sweet young voice will say, 'Is Danny Orlis there?' I tell you, it must be serious."

His cheeks flushed. "We're just good friends, that's all."

"Now don't try to tell me that." His roommate saw that he was getting a reaction from Danny and kept on, only his eyes smiling. "But I can tell you this much, we're all glad you're here. Now maybe we can do something else except answer the phone for you."

"Maybe I'd better get in touch with her, if she's so anxious to talk to me as all of that."

"It might be a good idea." When Danny was out in the hall, John stopped him with a word. "I guess I ought to tell you that she really only called for you once."

"That's more like it."

"But she sure sounded as though she wanted to talk to you about something. I told her we didn't even know whether you'd be back. None of us had heard from you since you left."

Danny called Kay. He really was anxious to talk to her, but he felt uncomfortable about it, too. She was always so sure about what she was to do. She would graduate from CBI and become a missionary. It was as simple as that. He didn't have such easy answers for the problems he had to face.

Danny borrowed a car from one of his friends that evening and took Kay to a little cafe on the edge of town where they had dinner. He had not fully realized how much he had missed her over the summer until now when they were together again or how much he enjoyed being with her.

They talked about their friends who had graduated the spring before and what they were doing and about the kids who were coming back. Kay seemed disturbed about those who weren't returning, as though their failure to come back was an indication of spiritual coldness. Danny found himself defending them.

"Maybe they've got good reasons for not going to school this year," he told her. "Did you ever stop to think of that?"

Her lips tightened and her eyes gleamed quizzically. He found himself squirming under her steady gaze.

"Yes, I have thought of that," she said. "And I know it's true that there are a lot of very good reasons why a person couldn't come back to school. But I was thinking of how they were last year. Quite a few of those who aren't back are the ones who were more concerned about having a good time than they were about studying. That's the thing that made me say what I did."

Danny changed the subject. "What kind of a summer did you have?"

Her smile winked saucily at him. "It was nice," she said, "but actually, it wasn't much different than the other summers I've spent in Mexico with Mom. We did the usual visiting in villages to tell Bible stories with pictures to the children and women and I taught a Bible class. I guess that's about the size of it."

"It sounds like a rewarding summer to me."

"Not as rewarding as you'd think. We were both somewhat disappointed with the results. Some of the girls and younger women have been so close to making a decision that Mom was sure they would come through this summer, but we didn't have a single conversion all three months."

Danny nodded. That was the way missionary work so often went, he understood from talking with some of the veterans who came to CBI to speak when they were back visiting in the States. This had been another reason he felt that he should forget about being a missionary and live on the Angle. He could do as much for the Lord working on the side at home as a lot of men who were full-time missionaries.

Kay broke the silence. "And what kind of a summer did you have, Danny?"

He shrugged. His summer had been a busy one, and bewildering. He was at CBI, but he still didn't have the answers to the problems that had been troubling him. While he was trying to decide what to say to her, the waitress came with their orders. Danny asked the blessing on the food and when he had finished, asked Kay about an important matter.

"Have you been doing any thinking about the kind of Christian service assignment you'd like to have?"

"I always do a lot of thinking about that," she answered. "I think I enjoy it as much as anything else here at school. I hope I get to work with high school kids in some way. It seems as though God has laid them on my heart more heavily than ever the last three months." She paused, eyes narrowing. "And what about you, Danny? What sort of Christian service assignment would you like to have?"

His cheeks flushed and he wished that he had never mentioned the subject. "I don't know, " he replied with growing uneasiness. "To tell you the truth, I haven't thought much about it yet. I guess it doesn't make a whole lot of difference. The important thing is to serve God. It doesn't matter much what you do."

Hurt leaped to her eyes. "But it does matter," she replied. "It matters a great deal. God may want you or me in one avenue of service. We can't expect Him to bless us if we ignore His leading and do something else."

"But Christian service assignments are made by the school without any regard for a student's leading by God."

Her gaze held his, forcibly. "That isn't what I meant," she replied, "and I didn't think that was what you meant, either, when you were talking just now about serving God."

"I'm sorry, Kay," he told her. "I guess I'm more interested right now in seeing whether I can find a job to pay my expenses in school this year than I am in what kind of a Christian service assignment I'm going to get. I didn't mean to get you all shaken up."

She sipped her tea thoughtfully. She could have misunderstood Danny. But it seemed to her that his remarks had slipped out as though he had opened the curtain of his mind briefly to let her see what was inside. If that were the case, it was disturbing. On the other hand, it could be that he had been preoccupied with thoughts of getting a job and hadn't said what he actually wanted to say. She was concerned about getting a job, too. Money was always a problem to missionary kids and she was no exception.

"To tell you the truth," she said aloud, "that's one of the chief reasons I wanted to get here a few days early. I thought I might be able to get a little better job than I would if I wait until everyone is here."

"I don't know for sure what I'll do if I'm not able to get a good paying job this year," he said, looking away. "I've told God that I'll go to school this year if He helps me to get a job that will pay well enough so I don't have to be a burden to Mom and Dad."

"Oh, you'll get the money you need," she told

him confidently. "Why don't we pray for each other about finding work?"

"That's a good idea," he replied.

The next morning Danny went to the school employment service to see what sort of jobs they had available. Miss Dickerson knew him and told him she was glad to have him back.

"It's good to be here," he murmured without enthusiasm.

She looked over the list quickly. "I'm sorry, Danny," she said. "We don't have a great deal to offer this semester. For some reason the requests for help have been awfully slow in coming in this year. It's been of some concern to us."

He was surprised how good that made him feel. Perhaps God had just been testing him to see if he would come back to school if that was His will for his life. Perhaps He didn't want him at CBI that year after all.

"I've got to have a job if I'm going to be able to go to school this year."

The graying staff member frowned and glanced over the list once more. "There isn't anything on this list that would give you enough hours to help substantially with your school expenses, Danny, but I've got a few leads that I'd like to chase down before we give up. I'll make a few phone calls and see if I can't find something for you."

Miss Dickerson told Danny to check back with her the next morning and that was what he planned to do, but she didn't wait until the next day. Shortly before five o'clock she called him to tell him the good news.

"God really must want you here this year," she said, excitedly. "I've found a job for you that I'm sure will be just what you want."

"You–you did?" he echoed weakly.

"It's not the most glamorous work in the world," she continued, "but I know you're not looking for something that's easy or carries a lot of prestige. It is a good-paying job and one that will fit any schedule ideally. You can decide when you want to work each day."

Danny felt his stomach tighten. He had been hoping fervently that nothing would develop.

"Is–is it something that I can do?" he asked.

"Oh, yes. You'll be doing janitor work at one of the Cedarton banks. Actually, I thought of the job when you were here, but I didn't want to say anything until I'd checked it out because I didn't want to get your hopes up. We had a student working there a year ago. He made enough to take care of his school expenses and still had a little left over for clothes and spending money."

"Thank you," he said weakly.

"You can come in tomorrow and get the card so you can be interviewed, but really that's just a formality. Their personnel officer said that CBI students have always been satisfactory so they would accept anyone we recommended to them."

Danny thanked her again. He would have to stay at CBI! He had asked God to show him what he should do. Now the answer was firm and clear. Still, disappointment surged within him. He really had wanted to spend that year on the Angle!

CHAPTER 3

RICK

Danny was glad that he didn't have a date with Kay that night. She would be excited about his job and thrilled with the way God answered prayer. At the moment he didn't think he could cope with her exuberance or with her calm assurance that God works everything out for good for those who love Him.

He was thrilled about the new job too, in a way. He knew now that this was God's will for his life and that he would have to stay at CBI if he were to remain in the center of God's will. And he was concerned about living for Him. It was just that he was so anxious to get back to the Angle where he could help his parents and do all of those things he had grown to enjoy so much as a kid. He had even been toying with the idea of getting out his traps and having a trapline again after the hunting season. Now all of that was out. He would be staying in school.

In spite of himself he had been excited about the job that had been offered to him. There were guys at CBI who would have given anything for a job like the one he had. As Miss Dickerson said, it wasn't glamorous, but it was better than cleaning bathrooms or lugging meat at the local packing plant or putting in long, weary hours at a service station in order to make expenses. Those were the kind of jobs some of the other guys had.

He would be expected to do his work, of course, and they would expect him to move briskly to get it done. But he wouldn't want it any other way. He wanted to work for what he got. He didn't want everything handed to him. It was important to him that he could set his own hours for each day, which allowed him to register for the classes he wanted and work his job around them. He could juggle his work time to fit the schedule of the day, exams, special assignments, and even parties, if he wished.

And a little mental arithmetic showed him that he would be able to meet all of his expenses and still have a bit left over. He would have to be careful about his spending but no more than anyone else.

He planned to wait until his date with Kay the next afternoon to tell her about the janitor job at the bank; but when he saw her in the dining room that evening, he went over and told her about it. She squealed with delight.

"And you were so concerned about it," she said.

"I knew you didn't have to be upset about not having a job. I knew that God was going to answer your prayers, and mine."

Kay paused as though debating whether to go on or not. "I don't know whether to tell you this or not, Danny, but last night when Ruth and I were praying you would find work, we both had the feeling that God was going to answer and in a way that was more wonderful than we could even hope for."

"Your prayers were answered," he told her. "And I want to thank you for them."

"Isn't it marvelous how God works?" she continued breathlessly. "He not only provided you with a job, but one that is ideal. In fact, it couldn't be better."

Danny nodded in agreement. The more he thought about it the stranger it seemed that he would get a job so much quicker than anyone else. And his job was good enough to meet his school expenses. He knew Miss Dickerson hadn't sought him out for that job because she particularly liked him above the other guys. She wouldn't have done that. It was really an answer to prayer. In that moment he wanted to ask Kay to pray that God would make him completely happy at school that year, but he did not. Instead he asked her whether she had found work or not.

"There are a few more jobs for girls than there are for boys," she said. "There's quite a lot of housework to do and a number of clerking jobs. I was out this afternoon being interviewed. I'm sure that something will turn up from one of them." Her smile was warm and lighthearted. "After what happened to you I know that God is going to help me find just the job He has for me too."

Danny and Kay were together often in the few days before school started. Once classes began, however, they had little time to be together. There were assignments to do, themes to write, and collateral reading to do in the library. And, of course, there were their jobs that also took time. It seemed that every hour of every day was taken up with something and they were fortunate to be able to get together once a week, except for an occasional chance meeting at the school post office or in the snack shop or dining room. Still, they were glad for those occasions.

It seemed to them as though they had not been apart that summer at all, but had taken up where they left off in May. It wasn't that they had decided to date only each other. They hadn't even discussed the matter of going out with others. Yet, neither of them went out with anyone else. They didn't care to.

There was a bond between them that neither could understand. Danny was relaxed and comfortable with Kay in a way that he had never been with anyone else, even his own family. And so it was with Kay. If she was blue and discouraged, she thought first of sharing the matter with Danny, drawing strength and comfort from the fact that he understood and cared. If she was happy and excited about something, he was the one she first wanted to tell. They had never spoken of love, but Danny had long had the feeling that someday he and Kay would be married. And he suspected from some of the things she said on occasion that she felt the same.

A few days after the semester opened at CBI, Danny and Kay were given their Christian service assignments. They were both pleased and excited about the work they would be doing for the coming semester.

Excitement danced in Kay's eyes as she told Danny about her responsibility.

"I couldn't have picked out a better assignment if I'd done it myself," she said. "It's going to be wonderful."

A grin tugged at the corner of his mouth. "I'm glad for that."

"I can still hardly believe it. You'll never guess what I'm going to be doing. I'm to help Marilyn Forester and Walt Sherman with one of the high school Bible clubs. Isn't that tremendous?"

Danny nodded. In a way it was an answer to prayer. On the other hand, anyone who knew Kay would have chosen her to work in the high school. She had enough bounce and spark to keep up with any teenager. And she had spiritual discernment and concern. She would be ideal for that job.

Danny was going to be helping with Christian Service Brigade at the church he was attending. He thought he would like that, too. He had enjoyed working with boys, and his experience on the Angle in hunting and fishing and woodcraft gave him the skills he needed to be an asset in the program.

But that didn't keep him from preferring to work with guys who were a little older than the Stockaders he was responsible for. He had always felt that he understood high school guys a little better and was able to do a little more with them. But he wasn't complaining. He could have been given an assignment in an old peoples' home or at the little rescue mission in town. He wouldn't have objected to either of the other assignments or to anything else, but he did prefer to work in a place where he had some special interest and enough experience to make it worthwhile for him. Besides, boys from eight to twelve years old were more responsive. He was glad for the opportunity of working with them.

* * *

Dewey Jensen, the youthful Christian education director, came to the first meeting and introduced Danny to the boys he would be working with.

"Now," he said, "I think Danny would like to know who you guys are. I'm going to ask you to stand in turn and give your name and the name of your parents." He turned to his left. "Tim, why don't we start with you? We'll go on down the line, one after the other, until you've all told Danny your name and your parents' names."

Tim Spaulding did as he was directed. When he sat down, the next stood and did the same, speaking loudly and clearly. At last they came to the final boy on the back row, a thin, spindling lad with a haunted look in his eyes.

"I–I'm Rick Henderson." He mumbled so softly it was difficult to catch his name. "And–"

Danny thought he saw the boy's lips tremble.

Rick stopped and began again, the words stumbling out. "I'm Rick Henderson and my mother's name is Esther–" He swallowed hard, and his cheeks flushed scarlet. "But–"

Danny sensed that Rick was from a broken home and that the boy was embarrassed by it.

"I'm certainly glad to know you, Rick," he said, striding forward and thrusting out his hand while the other Stockaders stared. "And I'm glad you're going to be in Stockade. We're going to need guys like you."

One of the boys in the front row snickered disdainfully, but Danny reproached him with a glance.

"We're going to make this the best Stockade in all of Minnesota. Now what do you think of that?"

Rick eyed him gratefully.

Then Danny glanced at the rest of the guys.

"To be truthful with you," he went on, "I'm glad to have all of you guys. I was just sitting here congratulating myself on getting to work with you. It's going to be great for me and I hope you like it, too."

The boys grinned at him.

"I didn't have a chance to take part in anything like this when I was a kid, and I always figured that I'd missed out on something. Now I'm going to be able to do something I've always wanted to do, be a part of Christian Service Brigade."

That was the first meeting of the fall season so there wasn't a great deal for anyone to do. They had a few games and sang some fun songs and choruses, and Danny gave them a short Bible lesson. When the meeting was over most of the boys went home, but Rick Henderson hung back, waiting uneasily not far from the door until everyone else was gone. Then he approached Danny hesitantly, embarrassment flushing his cheeks. He stood there for an agonizing moment before Danny saw him and spoke.

"I'm sorry, Rick. I didn't notice you standing there. Is there something I can do for you?"

The boy swallowed trying to rid himself of the lump in his throat. "I guess it isn't important."

He turned and would have left if Danny hadn't stopped him. "If it's important to you, it's important to me," he answered. "Let's go over and sit down so we can talk."

But Rick shook his head vigorously. "My mom'll skin me alive if I don't come right home. It won't take that long. I–I was just wondering something."

"Like what?"

"Could I–uh–have your telephone number?" he asked, "just in case I want to call you about some brigade stuff some time?"

"I don't see why not," Danny replied, fishing a scrap of paper from his pocket. "Here, I'll write it down for you so you won't forget it."

Rick took the paper with the phone number, studied it momentarily, and shoved it into his pocket.

"Thanks, Danny. Thanks a lot." His smile flashed and a moment later he was out the door and gone.

Dewey came over to where Danny was standing.

"I couldn't help noticing the way you handled Rick Henderson, Danny," he said. "I think you made a friend of him and that's more than I've been able to do."

"He looks as though he needs a friend."

"You can say that again. I gathered that you sensed the fact that his parents are separated, from the way you handled that introduction."

"I figured that must be it."

"His dad ran away with a barmaid five or six months ago, and I'm afraid his mother is taking out her frustration and bitterness on Rick. And he's as unhappy and as lonely as she is. It's made things real difficult for Rick."

Danny picked up his jacket. "I hope we can reach him for Christ."

"So do I. If we don't do it soon, I'm afraid he'll be spending some time in the boys' reform school. He's already been picked up for stealing from cars on the streets at night. One more offense and I'm afraid the judge will figure he has no course of action except to send him away for a year or so."

Danny walked slowly home through the warm September night air. He hadn't even suspected there would be anyone in Stockade with problems like that. It would be a challenge to work with Rick.

That night he spent a long time in prayer for the unhappy boy he had just met. And when he got to his feet, he scribbled Rick's name on a piece of paper and shoved it in his pocket so he would remember to ask Kay to pray for him.

CHAPTER 4

FRICTION ON EVERY HAND

At church the following Sunday morning, a well-dressed woman of thirty-five or forty came whisking up to Danny.

"Are you Mr. Orlis?" she asked crisply.

"I am." Curiosity gleamed in his eyes.

"The pastor pointed you out to me. I wonder if I could talk with you for a moment or two?"

"Right now?" He glanced at Kay, who was with him.

"I'll wait in the foyer," she told him.

"The pastor said we could use his study." She turned her attention to Kay briefly. "This won't take but a minute. I have a little matter I'd like to talk over with your friend."

Danny followed her into the pastor's study and closed the door behind them. "Won't you have a chair?"

The corners of her mouth tightened. "No, thank you. I can talk better standing up."

He waited for her to continue.

"I understand from my son that you are the new leader of Christian Service Brigade for the younger boys?"

"That's right. We had our first meeting a week ago."

She nodded. "My son was there. He also tells me that Richard Henderson was there, too."

"Oh yes, Rick was there," he answered.

"I thought you would remember him. You singled him out for special commendation."

At first Danny couldn't remember what she was talking about.

"Oh yes," he said after a moment. "I remember now. He was terribly embarrassed and I tried to set him at ease. I wasn't aware that I singled him out for any sort of commendation, though. I told him I was glad to have him in Stockade, that we needed him."

"That's just it!" She drew herself up, eyes flashing. "You're in school so you would have no way of knowing, but that boy is a thief!" She spat out the word contemptuously.

"I was talking with Mr. Jensen about him," Danny went on. "He tells me that Rick is a lonely, unhappy little boy who has gotten into trouble. He seems to feel that we can do something for him in Stockade."

"Do you mean to tell me that you are going to keep him in the group when you know what he's done? Are you going to let him associate with decent boys who might be influenced by him?"

Danny hesitated. He knew that there could be a

danger in keeping a youthful delinquent in a group like Stockade providing he had a strong personality and the other boys followed. But that wasn't the case with Rick. He was a lone wolf and so shy that nobody else would ever be influenced to do anything because of him. Danny felt like asking her if she had ever met the boy and talked with him. But he did not.

"What are you suggesting that I do?" he asked.

Her voice raised. "The least you can do is to tell that boy he isn't welcome at Stockade until he confesses his sin and becomes a Christian."

"Have you talked this over with the pastor?"

"He's as stubborn as you are. He wouldn't do a thing about it. He tried to tell me that the church is for people like Rick Henderson. But I expected you to be more reasonable."

"As far as I'm concerned, this is a church matter. There's nothing I can do about it."

Her eyes flashed. "You mean there's nothing you *will* do about it!"

Danny did not answer her.

"I thought you would be more understanding. After all, you're a Bible school student. You ought to be concerned about the souls of the boys you are working with."

"I am," he replied mildly. "And one of those souls is Rick Henderson."

She flounced out of the study and slammed the door.

The pastor caught Danny in the foyer. "I'm sorry

about Mrs. Wentworth, Danny," he said. "She told me she wanted to talk with you about her son being in Stockade, and I thought she was concerned about his spiritual condition. I didn't know she was going to tear into you about Rick Henderson. If I had, I'd have joined you."

"Who told you we were talking about Rick?" Danny wanted to know. "Could you hear us?"

"Oh, no." The pastor laughed. "I saw it in her eyes when she came tearing out of the study. And, from the way she looked, I gathered that she didn't get the satisfaction she thought she would get from you."

Danny talked with Kay about the matter on the way back to the school for dinner.

"She had no place in coming to me," he said. "I'm not even a member of the church. I'm just helping out this school term. It's up to the church to decide a matter like that."

She nodded. "But I'm glad you stood your ground just the same. That poor boy needs help, not another kick in the teeth."

"I just hope that's the end of it," he replied uneasily.

"It will be. People like Mrs. Wentworth usually back off when they don't get what they want."

Danny hoped that would be the way it went, but he wasn't so sure.

He half expected the woman to talk with him after the service that night or to call him at school the following day, but he didn't hear from her. By the time of the next Stockade meeting he had practically forgotten it.

As soon as Danny reached the church on Stockade night, Rick Henderson came over to him, smiling hesitantly as though he couldn't believe that Danny was still his friend.

"Hi," he said. "Do you remember me?"

"Sure I do." He reached out and rumpled the boy's hair. "You're Rick Henderson."

The thin-faced boy's grin widened slightly. "I was going to call you last night to find out if you were going to be here today, but my mom wouldn't let me. She said I shouldn't bother you."

"You should mind your mother, Rick, but it won't hurt for you to phone me once in a while."

The boy was relieved. "You mean it would be all right for me to tell her that I can call you up once in a while – whenever I've got some question to ask about something in Stockade?" he wanted to know.

"Sure. You can tell her that I said it would be all right for you to phone me once in a while. I like to have my friends call me."

Something close to adoration flecked the boy's eyes.

It seemed to Danny that Rick spent the rest of the evening looking at him. Whenever he glanced in Rick's direction, Rick was studying him seriously. It was somewhat uncomfortable to feel those haunted eyes fastened on him so tightly. But it was gratifying, too.

"At least I'm beginning to build some rapport with him, Kay," Danny told her over a dish of ice cream in the snack shop the next day. "I've never seen a kid quite like him. He seems to be starved for affection and love."

"You have a tremendous opportunity to reach him for Christ, Danny," she said. "If he thinks so much of you, he'll really listen when you tell him that Christ loves him and wants to save him."

He paused for a moment.

"It goes to show that there are all sorts of opportunities to serve God right here at home, doesn't it?"

Something in his tone disturbed her.

"What do you mean by that, Danny?"

"I was just thinking about the people back on the Angle," he continued. "Those who live there and those who come to fish and hunt. There would be a wonderful place right there to witness for Christ."

"Unless God is calling one somewhere else," she told him.

His cheeks darkened uncomfortably. "Now I've got to ask you what you mean," he said.

Once she had opened the subject, Kay continued bravely. "I was thinking of that time last year when you made a decision to dedicate your life to God and you said that you felt led to the mission field. When you spoke the way you did just now, I couldn't help wondering if you were trying to tell me that you had changed your mind and wanted to go back to the Angle to live when you finish school?"

Danny was a long while in answering. "I really don't know what I want to do," he said, shrugging. "I've done a lot of thinking about it, but I haven't come to a definite decision."

"That sounded quite definite to me," she told him quietly.

"All I did was make a remark that there are a lot of people right here in the United States who need to be challenged with the gospel of the Lord Jesus Christ." Now that they were talking about it, he felt that he had to continue, to explain exactly how he felt. "I'll admit that I have thought seriously about going back to the Angle to help Dad and to witness to the people I come in contact with. There wouldn't be anything wrong with that, would there?"

"No," Kay said. "Not if that is actually where God wants you to be."

They began to talk about other things, but it seemed to Danny as though their time together had been ruined, that there was a blight that choked off conversation. He was still disturbed about it when he went up to his room to study.

During the days that followed, Danny didn't have an opportunity to talk with Rick Henderson alone about his need for confessing his sin and taking Christ as his Savior, but there were times when he wondered if he had done the right thing in giving the boy his phone number and allowing him to tell his mother that it was all right for him to call.

He took to telephoning at all hours, most of them inconvenient for Danny, to ask some sort of a question about Stockade.

"What time does the meeting start tomorrow night, Danny?" he would ask. Or "What should I bring besides my handbook?"

"You've really got a buddy," John said when Danny came back to their room after talking with Rick. "He calls you oftener than Kay, doesn't he?"

"You can say that again."

"Doesn't it bug you to have him bother you all the time? It would sure get to me, I can tell you."

"I guess there are times when I wish he wasn't quite so friendly with me."

The instant Danny said that he was sorry. He really didn't dislike Rick, and he didn't mind the calls all that much. It was just that there were times when he was busy and the interruptions were irritating. Actually, he liked Rick immensely and had a real burden for him.

He knew how alone the fatherless lad must feel. Other boys could talk about their dads helping them with one project or another, but he couldn't. He had to get his help from his mother or from a friendly neighbor. And when they had a father's night, which the church insisted on occasionally, he didn't have anyone to bring with him. Danny could easily understand why Rick needed someone older to talk to. And he was glad for the opportunity to help him.

The attitude of the other kids toward Rick might have been a little different if he hadn't been so poor and if he had been good at sports. He was one of those kids who couldn't hang onto a basketball or run across the floor without falling down. Nobody wanted him on their team when it came to playing any kind of a game.

"Oh, do we have to have *him?*" Bill Wentworth demanded.

"Rick's on your team," Danny told him evenly.

The Henderson boy cringed.

"My mother said–" Bill began petulantly.

But Danny cut him off short. "Come on, let's get the game started."

Rick tried as hard as he could, but he cost his team two points and the game. The guys all groaned their dismay.

"It's not fair," one of them blurted. "We shouldn't have to have Rick on our team if we don't want him."

Danny debated calling the rest of the Stockade together without Rick and talking with them about him, trying to get them to understand how lonely he was and how much he needed help. But he wasn't sure that was the thing to do. Guys that age could be terribly cruel. He was afraid they would get the idea that he was favoring Rick, and that would only make the matter worse.

CHAPTER 5

BROKEN ROMANCE

Danny and Kay saw each other as much as ever during the next few weeks, but a thin, almost invisible barrier had come between them, a barrier that dulled every date and strained every conversation. They were still friends but they were also strangers, separated by something they did not quite understand. Danny sensed it and tried to push it aside or to pretend that it was not there, but he was only deceiving himself.

It seemed worse when Kay talked about missions and being led to serve God on the mission field. Danny cringed inwardly when that happened and tried to change the subject as quickly as possible.

"What's wrong?" Kay blurted on one occasion. "Aren't you interested in missions anymore?"

He managed a twisted smile. "Sure, I'm interested in missions. You ought to know that by this time.

How can anyone be around CBI as long as we have and not be interested in missions?"

Her gaze held his. "That isn't exactly what I mean," she replied. "Are you interested in missions personally, as a field of service, if God leads you in that way?"

"Of course I am," he told her almost belligerently. "I've already told you that. I'm interested in being a missionary if that's what God wants me to be. I'm just not convinced yet that He's leading in that direction."

Kay said no more about it, but she was still hurt and more disturbed than ever by Danny's attitude. They went on to the concert, but she didn't enjoy it very much. When it was over, she had a headache and asked Danny to take her home. He knew the reason, she was sure; but he didn't mention it and neither did she. It was one of those things that talking didn't seem to help.

For the next month or so they both carefully avoided the subject, but it was never far from Kay's thoughts. There were times after they had been together when she found it almost impossible to sleep, her thoughts and emotions churned so violently.

She had never actually considered being anything other than a missionary since she had been a little girl. She didn't know why, but it had always seemed the only thing for her. Even after her dad died in Mexico, she had not wavered in that decision. It probably was stronger if that were possible.

Kay had always assumed that someday she and Danny would be married and serve God together.

She felt that had been one of the reasons God had led her up to Cedarton, Minnesota, for high school and to CBI. It had seemed as though they were meant for each other. Now, however, she began to wonder whether she ought to keep dating him or not.

There had been a marked change in Danny since school started, a change so marked that there were times when she wondered whether he was even the same person. He seldom mentioned his Christian service assignment anymore, except to complain about Rick Henderson who called him so constantly and kept wanting to come over and see him.

Complaining about something like that wasn't like Danny. She would have expected him to be happy about the boy's liking him and wanting to be with him. The year before he would have looked on it as an opportunity rather than a burden.

Kay couldn't help comparing him with Walt Sherman who worked with her in the high school Bible club. Walt had difficulty in talking about anything else and was thrilled when one of the kids called him or stopped to talk to him on the street. She continued to pray for Danny and their relationship with each other.

* * *

Danny Orlis stood in the doorway of the boys' dorm that afternoon watching Kay and Walt Sherman cross the parking lot together and get into Walt's car. They were talking and laughing with a joy that seldom marked Danny's dates with her. They were only going to their Christian service assignment. He knew that. Still, jealousy wrenched at his heart.

He wouldn't have thought so much about it if things were still the same between him and Kay. But they weren't. He still thought as much of her as ever, and he thought she had a special place in her heart for him. He had thought that, at least, until now.

As Kay and Walt drove away, Danny couldn't help wondering if she was getting interested in her companion. This was Bible school, and that sort of thing happened often here. A couple was paired for a Christian service assignment or in a singing group and before long they were interested in each other. But on occasion, someone else was badly hurt by it.

He wished he could talk frankly with her about it, but he didn't feel that he could. The last few weeks they had grown apart until they were almost like strangers at times. He went back to his room and tried to study, but he couldn't keep his mind on anything. All he could think about was Kay and the fact that he might be losing her.

Had it not been for that he probably wouldn't have been so disturbed when Rick called and wanted to come over.

"I've been working on this badge, Danny," the boy said, "and I don't know whether I'm doing it right or not. I wondered if I could come over and let you tell me if I'm doing OK."

"Does it have to be done tonight?" Danny asked irritably. "We'll be having our meeting in a couple of nights. I can help you then."

Rick was hurt by his lack of friendliness. "I guess I can wait," he said, "but I sort of wanted to have it finished by then."

Danny started to tell him that he couldn't take the time because he had to study, but he realized that wasn't true. He didn't want to see Rick because he was upset about Kay and didn't want to listen to the boy's chatter.

"All right, Rick," he said. "Come on out this evening and I'll take a look at it. OK?"

The boy brightened. "Do you mean it's all right for me to come out to the school and see you?" he asked. "Can I come to the dorm?"

"That's right. Come to the boys' dorm and have the guy at the desk call me. I'll come right down and get you."

"Oh boy! That's great! Thanks, Danny. Thanks a lot!"

Rick rode his bike out to the school that evening and came up to Danny's room with him, eyes wide with excitement.

"This is great!" He turned impulsively to Danny. "I think I'll come out here to college when I grow up."

Talking with Rick that evening took longer than Danny thought it would. The boy hadn't had much to see him about, actually. Danny suspected that he had opened his handbook after the phone conversation and grabbed a badge that he thought he should be working on. He asked all sorts of silly questions about the requirements. More than once Danny wanted to stop him and send him home. At last, however, shortly after nine o'clock, Rick got reluctantly to his feet.

"I guess I'd better go, Danny," he murmured. "Thanks for letting me come out and see you."

Danny smiled.

"I was supposed to go out with a couple of other guys tonight, but I told them that I'd rather come and see you."

"I'm glad you came," Danny replied without enthusiasm. It was good to have the boy's admiration, but at times it was a little wearing.

He followed Rick downstairs and to the front door.

"My mom has a date tonight," the boy explained lamely, "so it doesn't matter when I get home."

Danny looked into Rick's eyes and suddenly he was ashamed of his own lack of concern for Rick. The boy was upset by this new development in his life, desperately lonely, and more than a little afraid. That was the reason he had come out to the school that night. He had to have someone to turn to.

"Why don't I see if I can borrow a car, Rick?" he asked impulsively. "If I can, you can leave your bike here tonight and we'll go have some ice cream and I'll take you home afterward. OK?"

* * *

It was shortly before ten o'clock when Danny went into the house with Rick, turned on the lights for him, and made sure that he knew how to lock the doors.

"I've got to run now," he said, "but I'm sure your mother will be home in a little while."

"Thanks, Danny," Rick said gratefully. "You sure would make a good dad for some kid."

Danny drove home thoughtfully. Rick would never know how that simple statement stung him. If only he had known how Danny felt when he called him and wanted to see him that night or how close he had come to sending him home. A good dad? He hadn't spent the evening with Rick because he wanted to. He'd done so because the boy was so insistent he hadn't been able to get rid of him. A year ago he wouldn't have been that way. Or would he? What was happening to him anyway?

Danny had lunch with Kay the next day and they went to a pizza shop for dinner that night.

"I hear you had company last night, Danny," she said.

"Yeah, I couldn't get out of it."

Her eyes narrowed. "I should think you'd be glad he has enough confidence in you to make him want to come and see you."

"I do, but it can get to be a drag." He didn't know why he had said that. He didn't honestly feel that way anymore. Perhaps it was because he was upset over their relationship or because he knew she wanted him to be excited about it and he resented it as an attempt to run his life. Whatever it was, he had succeeded in striking her in a vulnerable place. He saw her wince.

It was then that Kay laid aside her fork and stared at him.

"This may not be the place for this, Danny," she said, "but we can't go on this way any longer."

He eyed her uneasily. "What do you want to talk about?" he demanded. "Walt Sherman?"

Her cheeks flushed: "Danny! Don't be like that!"

"What else is there to talk about? We got along fine until he came along. Now that the two of you are spending so much time together I'm suddenly a rascal who never does anything right."

"Danny, please don't make this any harder than it is," she murmured, tears trembling on her eyelashes.

He lowered his voice. "All right. What is it that you want to talk to me about?"

"Last spring," she said, "you made a decision to consecrate your life to Christ."

"That's right. That's the reason I'm here at CBI this year instead of at home helping Dad, where I'm really needed."

Kay had difficulty in forming the words. "You know that I feel led to the mission field, don't you?"

He nodded. He ought to know it, he told himself. She had reminded him often enough.

"Last spring you talked about the mission field,

too, as though that was your goal and purpose in life. But this year you act as though you've changed your mind. I get the impression that you are turning your back on the mission field. Is that right?"

"I want to follow God's leading," he told her, defensively, "but I'm not sure that the mission field is involved in it. I've been concerned about the area right around home. I think I could do a real work for God right on the Angle and still be able to be where I want to be and do the things I want to do."

Kay folded her hands tightly on the table in front of her to keep them from trembling. "That's what I was afraid of."

"Afraid of?" he echoed. "The lost and uncommitted are all around us. I feel the Angle would be just as much of a mission field as Africa or New Guinea or Mexico."

"I do, too," she replied. "And I would feel that is the place you should serve – if it is where God is leading you."

"I'm beginning to believe that it is," he said. "I know the country and the people. I'd be able to be an effective witness where I might not be able to do more than put in time somewhere else."

It was two or three minutes before Kay spoke. When she did, her voice trembled so much he could scarcely understand her.

"I–I can't begin to tell you how hard it is for me to say this, Danny, but I–I don't think we ought to be together anymore."

He drew in his breath sharply, as though she had struck him a sledgehammer blow in the pit of the stomach.

"What do you mean?" he asked weakly.

"I don't feel that we ought to be dating as long as God is leading me toward the mission field and you feel that you should serve Him here in America."

Danny's mind reeled. It couldn't be true. There had to be some terrible mistake, a cruel joke someone was trying to pull on him. But it wasn't. He read the hurt in her eyes and the determination mingling with it.

This was no quick decision, he knew. She wasn't suddenly angry about something and flaring up at him. She had spoken only after long and careful deliberation. She had definitely made up her mind. There would be no changing her! A great, chilling void engulfed him.

CHAPTER 6

MORE TROUBLE

Danny said no more to Kay until they had finished eating and were outside. Then he tried to talk with her seriously, to make her understand that he was concerned about letting God have His way with his life and that she ought to keep on dating him.

"We've both got the same desires and purposes for our lives," he told her. "There's no reason why we shouldn't be together."

But it was impossible to reason with her. Her mind was made up and there was no changing it. Tears coursed down her cheeks and her voice broke again and again as she tried to explain her reasons for deciding they shouldn't date any more.

"I've been thinking about this and praying about it since shortly after school started this fall, Danny," she told him. "It's best that we don't date any more, at least until we know exactly the direction in which

God is leading you." He reached over and took her hand in his. She made no effort to pull away.

"Don't you want to go with me?" he asked quietly.

"You know better than to ask that, Danny." There was a new seriousness in her voice. "That's the reason it's been so difficult for me to make up my mind about this."

He shook his head incredulously. "If that's true, why won't you go out with me anymore?"

"Don't you understand?" she asked, her voice trembling. "I can't!"

Danny's anger surged. Why did she have to be so difficult? She was making a problem where there wasn't any, insisting that they break up when there was no real reason for it. They weren't engaged. They hadn't even committed to each other. And besides, they still had a year and a half of Bible school. A lot of things could happen in a year and a half. Kay might feel entirely different about going out as a missionary by the time she graduated.

She might have a hangup about missions because her parents were missionaries and her dad died on the field. Maybe her mother had been doing a lot of talking to influence her. That didn't sound much like Mrs. Milburn, he had to admit, but she might have done it without even being aware of it. And Kay might not be aware of the reason for wanting to become a missionary, either. If that was the case, the chances were that she would change her mind before they got out of school.

But by that time it would be too late.

He could change his thinking, too. Maybe he would feel led to become a missionary after all and would make application to go to some foreign field. He supposed it could happen.

There were so many things that were uncertain at that point. Didn't she realize that they could always break up if that seemed to be the thing to do? It didn't have to be done now–before either of them was in a position to make a definite decision about anything.

Danny took Kay back to the girls' dorm and told her good-bye. For a long moment she clung to his arm almost convulsively. Hope came flooding back that she was changing her mind. But only for an instant.

"I'm terribly sorry, Danny," she murmured, almost under her breath. "Good-bye."

He watched her disappear slowly into the girls' dorm, then turned and crossed the campus to the building that was the boys' dorm. He brushed past two guys in the lounge without speaking to them and hurried up to his room. John was there studying.

"Say, that was either a short date or it's later than I think," his roommate said.

No answer.

John pushed his chair half around and stared at Danny. "Why so glum? Did you and Kay have a fight or something?"

"Not exactly." Anger flecked Danny's voice.

"Take it easy," John countered with the bluntness

of a good friend. "I was just kidding you. That's no cause to bite my head off."

"I'm sorry." Danny sat down and stared at the wall.

For a minute silence echoed in the room. At last John spoke.

"Is it something you would like to tell me about?" he asked gently, "or would you rather sit there and go quietly out of your mind?"

"I'm sort of shaken up right now," Danny said, "but I guess I'd just as well tell you about it. The whole school will know by tomorrow, anyway."

"You must've broken up with Kay."

"How did you know?"

"A guy wouldn't exactly have to be a mind reader to know that. After a date with her you come storming in here like a tornado with no place to go. It's just got to have something to do with her."

"It does," Danny said numbly. "We're not together anymore."

John frowned. "That's too bad. Is it Walt Sherman?"

"She says it isn't."

"Well, if she's not dating anyone else it might not be too serious. You can probably see her in a day or two and get everything patched up."

"Oh no, this is for keeps. She's been thinking about it and praying about it for weeks." He told John what was troubling Kay. "I tried my best to make her see that she's getting all uptight a year and a half too soon. But it doesn't do any good to try to reason with her. She's got her mind made up."

John took a small notebook from his shirt pocket and began to finger it thoughtfully. "She might have a good reason, at that, Danny. You know a lot of potential missionaries get off the track because they fall in love and want to marry someone who isn't headed in that direction."

Danny's anger flamed. "Who's side are you on, anyway?"

"Wait a minute!" John exclaimed. "This is where I came in." With that he turned back to his books, leaving Danny sitting there studying the pattern of the tile at his feet.

Although Kay had been the one to break off going out with Danny, she was as upset as he was about it. Naturally the story spread around school and the girls all had to ask about it, lavish in their sympathy for her. Some of them understood why she had to do what she did; some of them didn't and tried to argue with her.

"You should adapt yourself to what Danny feels he is led to do," one friend told her. "The Bible says that the woman's place is to go with her husband."

"But he's not my husband," Kay reminded her.

"You ought to keep on dating him and try to persuade him to change his mind about the mission field," another girl suggested. "After all, if you really think a lot of him, and I know you do, you want him to follow the Lord's leading."

Kay didn't try to argue with them. She wasn't sure that she could answer their arguments, for one thing. They made their points of view sound so logical, so right. And, for another, it hurt too much to talk about it. It was easier for her if she shoved the entire matter back into the inner recesses of her mind so she could pretend for a little while that the problem didn't exist.

But, regardless of what she did, she continued to think about Danny. Every place she went and practically everything she did made her think about him. They had spent so much time together and had done so many things together that there were memories everywhere.

She cried herself to sleep more often than she cared to admit. But nobody, not even her roommate, knew about that. She turned her pillow over in the morning, quickly, so Ruth wouldn't see that the pillowcase was moist with tears.

During that period she found Walt Sherman more comfort and help than he knew. They always rode together to Bible club and spent time together on other occasions during the week to plan the meetings and talk about the things they were going to do. He was interesting to be with and she enjoyed his company a great deal. She thought of him more as a brother than a boyfriend.

Walt knew that Danny and Kay had broken up, but he wasn't aware that she was so upset about it. When he saw that she was upset about something, he persuaded her to go out with him for a pizza after Bible club.

"I really shouldn't," she told him. "I've got loads of studying to do."

"You can study when we get back. Maybe you'll feel more like it and get a lot more done."

"It could be, at that."

Across the table from her he mentioned the troubled look in her eyes. "You act as though you're carrying the whole world on your shoulders."

"Maybe I am." Her smile came slowly.

"You're too pretty for a load like that. Why don't you share it with someone?"

"I have," she told him significantly.

At first he didn't understand. "Oh," he said at last. "Oh, yes. But, aside from praying about it, why don't you talk it over with me? It might help, you know."

"You really wouldn't be interested, Walt," she told him, wishing he would talk about something else.

"How about trying me and finding out?"

She faced him. "There isn't any problem bothering me right now, Walt. It was a personal matter that bothered me a great deal until God gave me the answer to it. I'm just getting over it now, that's all."

He realized, then, that the problem was Danny. He couldn't understand why she would feel that way and still break up with the guy, but he had been around girls enough to know there were a lot of things about them that he didn't understand. He didn't ask Kay for a date right then, but he promised himself that he wasn't going to wait too long until he did. Somebody else might beat him to it.

* * *

Danny didn't know when Mrs. Wentworth decided to take her son out of Stockade. Bill didn't say anything to him about quitting. He simply didn't come any more. When he missed three meetings in a row, the pastor suggested that Danny call on him.

"That's not going to be easy, you know," he said, looking at the card that had been handed him.

The minister nodded. "I'm sure it won't be. His mother was at the last board meeting to protest the fact that we still allow Rick Henderson to come to Brigade. She didn't like it when they refused to do anything, either. I've been expecting something like this."

"If that's the way things are," Danny answered, "why don't we forget about calling on Billy? We'll just get a lot of static."

"We can't do that. Billy is important to the Lord too."

At the next Stockade meeting Danny called a couple of Billy Wentworth's best friends aside and asked about him.

"I don't think he's coming anymore," one of them said.

"Why not?" As if he had to ask.

"His mom didn't want him to."

Danny flinched. That was what he had expected. Mrs. Wentworth had as much as told him she would pull her son out of the organization if Rick was allowed to come. She was just making good on it.

If he were to do what he thought best, he wouldn't even see the boy. After having talked with the boy's mother, he knew it would be useless. But the pastor had asked him to, and he knew that he would be expected to make a report in a few days. So he got a friend to take him to Billy's school about the time classes were out in the afternoon. He caught the boy going across the street with a couple of other boys his own age.

Danny had his friend stop and he called to Billy. The boy said something in an undertone to his companions and came swaggering over to the car.

"I suppose you want to talk to me about Stockade," he said, his voice revealing his arrogance.

"What makes you think that?"

"My mom told me you'd probably be coming around to find out why I haven't been coming."

"As a matter of fact, I have missed you."

"Mom said to tell you that I can come back when that Rick Henderson is kicked out, and not before."

"I'm sorry, Billy."

"And she said to tell you that it won't do any good for you to come and see her, either. Her mind is made up."

The boy knew the conversation was over and turned to strut back to his companions.

"What was that all about?" the student who was driving the car asked Danny.

"It's a long story." He made a notation on the card. He wouldn't have to see Mrs. Wentworth now, that was one thing, but he wasn't happy about it. How did a guy get in such a mess as this when he was only trying to serve the Lord?

On the way back to the school he told his friend what had happened.

"You know, I feel more sorry for Billy than I do for Rick."

Danny had to admit that he did too.

CHAPTER 7

A CONFLICT WITH POLICE

A week or so after Walt took Kay out for a pizza, he asked her to go with him again, this time to dinner on Friday night and to a concert afterward.

She hesitated momentarily. She didn't want to hurt Walt's feelings. After all, he had been very good to her. But she didn't care to go with him. She really didn't care to go with anyone except Danny. That was all over now, however. She had to forget about him.

It would surely be better to go with a nice guy like Walt than to sit around the dorm, lonely and feeling sorry for herself. And Walt was the type of person she would want to date. He had a strong Christian testimony, a lively sense of humor, and a quick, inquiring mind. It was stimulating just to be with him. Under other circumstances she knew she would have been eager to go with him. Finally she agreed.

"That sounds like fun."

"Fine. I'll pick you up at six thirty on the dot. What do you think of that?"

She laughed happily.

Danny found out about Kay's date with Walt Sherman on his way to work Saturday morning. The guys he rode to town with told him about it. He cringed inwardly, but he couldn't let them know about it.

"I don't know why you'd think I'm interested in what she does or doesn't do," he replied. "I don't have any strings on her and she doesn't have any on me. We're not even together anymore."

"I just thought you'd like to know," the driver told him.

Danny was on the verge of answering rudely, but he managed to control himself. He didn't want it getting back to Kay that he was all broken up because she'd had another date. Things were bad enough without having her think that he was brokenhearted at losing her.

He had known all along that it was going to happen sooner or later, and he figured it would be with Walt Sherman. They were together a lot, for one thing. And for another she always talked about Walt as though she enjoyed his company a great deal.

If she had to date, he was glad it was with a nice guy like Walt. At least she was going out with a boy who would treat her the way she should be treated. Still, that didn't make him feel any better about the fact that someone else was taking his place with her. The hours dragged endlessly that day and when night came he was exhausted – too exhausted to even study.

At church the following morning, Danny met Kay in the foyer. She smiled warmly and came over to him.

"Hello, Danny."

"Hi." He found it difficult to speak to her.

"It's been so long since I've seen you," she said softly.

The muscles about his mouth tightened and his eyes glittered narrowly. "I understand that you haven't been lonesome."

She recoiled at the sudden anger of his voice. Her lips parted as though she was about to speak, and he thought he saw tears quivering on her eyelashes. Then, silently she turned and hurried inside, leaving him alone.

He ached inwardly, and for an instant, debated leaving the church that morning so he wouldn't have to sit there knowing she was in the same service. In the end he remained, but he didn't get much out of the message. When he got home, he couldn't even remember the passage of scripture the pastor had read, let alone the message.

Kay was as desirable as ever to Danny, he had to admit. Perhaps even more desirable than before, now that they were no longer together.

He sat at his desk, thoughtfully. There was only one thing standing between them, according to what she told him when she said she couldn't go with him anymore. That was his determination to go back to the Angle and live, while she planned to go out as a missionary.

It wasn't an insurmountable problem, he told himself. He had thought a little about the mission field as an avenue of Christian service. While he had decided against it, life wouldn't be much, even on his beloved Angle, without Kay. He guessed he could go out as a missionary for Kay's sake. She meant that much to him.

But even as the thought came, he realized that he couldn't do it. In the first place it wouldn't be honest. If he decided to become a missionary, it had to be because God was leading him in that direction, and not because Kay, or anyone else wanted him to. He had seen a number of kids at Bible school who were caught up in the excitement of the mission field and made decisions without any definite commitment or leading from God. They were stirred by the messages of returned missionaries and felt the lure of adventure and faraway places. They were sincere Christian kids, too, but they seldom got as far as the mission field and if they did, they only lasted one term. He didn't want that and neither would Kay.

It had to be genuine. It had to come from the deep conviction that he was doing exactly what God wanted him to do. That was enough to stop him, even though he really longed to be led in that direction so he could be with Kay again. He prayed a great deal about it, but there seemed to be no answer.

During the next two or three weeks Danny spent more time studying and at the bank working than he had ever spent before. At last he wearied of that and began to look around for something else to do.

Out of sheer loneliness he decided to date someone himself. He had no thought of making Kay jealous or of showing her that he could get someone else to go with him. He didn't feel particularly attracted to the girl he asked to go out with him. She was attractive enough, and he did think he would enjoy her company, but that was all.

Joan Gunderson hesitated before answering him.

"Is it true that you've broken up with Kay?" she asked.

"That's one way of putting it. To be honest with you, she's the one who broke up with me."

"I see." Her smile winked pleasantly at him.

"I have heard that you've broken up, of course. I suppose everyone at CBI has heard it. And I know the reason. I just wanted to be sure that the two of you weren't back together again."

"Fat chance of that," he muttered.

"I don't know. You two always seemed so 'right' for each other."

Joan said she would go out with him, and they agreed on a time. In spite of the fact that they both tried hard to make the date a success, the evening dragged on and they were glad when it was over. Danny didn't ask to take her out again and she wouldn't have gone with him if he had.

Danny tried to occupy his time with his Christian service assignment. He had a party and a cookout for his Stockaders in addition to their regular activities and visited the homes of the boys who had stopped coming or who were irregular in their attendance. He even went to see Billy Wentworth's mother about letting him come back to Stockade, although he expected, and got, a bitter refusal.

There was always Rick Henderson.

He would take up all the time Danny wanted to give him, and then some. After the first time Danny invited him out to the dorm, the boy was quick to find excuses to come out again. Danny couldn't help feeling sorry for him. His mother was going with some guy and was never home at night, so most of the time Danny let him come out although he grumbled about it to his roommate.

"Rick's coming out again tonight," he said one Friday evening, "so I suppose I'll be listening to his chatter for two or three hours."

John pulled on his shoes and tied them. He had a date that evening and it was getting time for him to go.

"I guess I made a mistake the first time when I told him that he could come out here and see me. He acts now as though he'd like to move in."

His roommate paused for a moment or two, and when he spoke his voice was distant and reminiscent of the past. "I don't know whether I told you this or not, but when I was Rick's age, I didn't have a dad either. He died when I was four years old. You know, I latched onto a neighbor kid up the block, a high school senior who took a liking to me. I'm sure I was as big a pest to him as Rick is to you, but I've never forgotten what he did for me."

Danny winced. He hadn't thought of it that way. That night when Rick came over he spent much more time with him than usual and ended by taking him out for some ice cream. Sitting in the cafe he took the opportunity to share the Lord Jesus Christ with Rick in a personal way. He had talked to him in general terms at Brigade meeting or, on one or two occasions, when the two of them were alone. This time, however, he made it personal.

"Have you ever thought about the fact that God loves you, Rick?" he asked.

The boy shook his head. "I guess I've never thought about it," he murmured.

"He does. He loves you so much that He wants to give you a new life." Danny went on to explain the way of salvation. He quoted Bible verses that proved that everyone was a sinner and separated from God for all eternity. He quoted other verses that showed that God had sent His only Son, Jesus Christ, into the world to live a sinless life and to die on the cross so Rick and everyone else who confessed his sin and put his trust in Jesus could be saved.

The boy didn't decide on anything but he listened intently and when Danny let him out at home shortly after ten o'clock, he was sure that Rick Henderson was thinking seriously about his own relationship with God and his need of confessing his sin and accepting Jesus Christ as his Savior. Danny spent a long while in prayer about it.

On Monday morning he was on his way to class when the Christian education director at the church came hurrying up to him.

"Oh, there you are, Danny. I've been looking all over for you."

He faced Dewey Jensen, smiling. "You look all uptight about something."

"I am." He spoke softly although there was no one else within a dozen paces or more. "Some of our Stockaders have gotten into real trouble. The pastor and I just came from the police station. He thought I should come and talk with you."

As they walked across the campus, the cold December wind whipping about them, Dewey told him what had taken place. Clark Poppe and Tod Crandall had been caught stealing from parked cars at the high school basketball game Friday night. A third boy was able to elude the police, but Clark and Tod both implicated Rick Henderson.

"Oh, no!" Danny's dismay was genuine.

"The other boys were remanded to the custody of their parents, but Rick's mother refused to accept the responsibility for him so it looks as though he's going to have to stay in jail until the trial."

"That's too bad," Danny replied. His first thought was to go down and see if he could sign for Rick, himself. If he did, he'd be able to get him out of jail for a while, at least. He couldn't stand to think of the boy having to stay in jail even for a few days. But what could he do about it? He couldn't assume responsibility for Rick and have him stay in the dorm. And the only way he could know what Rick was doing would be to have him live with him. In this, he was helpless.

"Is there something I can do?" he asked aloud.

"Rick is so shaken up and so afraid of having to go to the reform school that he's terribly upset. We thought perhaps you could go and see him."

"Sure, I can do that. I'll go this afternoon in my first free period."

Dewey paused significantly. "We thought perhaps you ought to go now. He keeps saying that he isn't guilty and that he wants to see you. It probably won't take too long, but it will be a tremendous help to him."

Danny caught a ride into Cedarton with the director of Christian education and they stopped at the jail where Rick was being held.

"Would you like to have me wait for you?" he asked.

"Better yet, why don't you come in with me?" Danny replied.

"I think it would be best if you talk with him alone."

They brought the boy up to a small office off that of the chief of police and Danny spoke to him. His voice caught as he saw Rick's tear-stained cheeks.

"You–you did come to see me," he stammered. "I didn't think you'd come, Danny."

"Of course I'd come. Why wouldn't I?"

Rick's lips curled bitterly. "Who'd want to come and see a guy who's in jail?"

Danny went over and put his arm about the boy's frail shoulder. For a moment Rick started to cry again, but that lasted only for a moment. He stood up tall and stared evenly at Danny.

"They won't believe me, but I didn't do it. I honestly didn't do it."

They went over and sat down across from each other.

"Would you like to tell me about it, Rick?" Danny asked quietly.

The boy paused.

"I don't know why those guys would say that I was with them. I didn't even see them after school Friday. I didn't know anything about it."

"You should tell the police that, Rick."

"I have, but they keep saying that they've got two guys who say it was me. And I've already been in that kind of trouble a couple of times. They won't believe anything I tell them."

Danny breathed deeply. He knew what Rick was talking about. And he couldn't blame the authorities. They had already caught him twice. Why should they believe him when he said that he wasn't guilty this time?

CHAPTER 8

THE PERFECT ALIBI

Danny went back to school after leaving the police chief's office, the heaviness in his heart growing. Rick's voice had the ring of truth when he said that he had not been in on the thefts. Yet he had to admit that he was suspicious too. The boy had been in trouble for the same offense. And the other boys hadn't been caught doing anything illegal. In fact, Danny didn't think they had ever been suspected of stealing or vandalism or anything else before that would attract the attention of the police. It did look as though Rick was the ringleader, as they said, and had been clever enough to get away from the officer who caught Clark and Tod.

Still, it didn't seem to square with what Danny knew about Rick's personality. He could see the boy stealing from cars or breaking windows in the schoolhouse or kicking in somebody's screen door alone, but he couldn't see him being in on anything like that with anyone else. And it was unthinkable that he would be the leader in an operation like that. The guys didn't even want to play ball with him on a team, let alone follow him in a gang of thieves. That didn't make sense at all.

Danny scarcely heard the lecture in his next class, so disturbed was he about Rick Henderson. When it was over and he went back to his room, he was still concerned about the boy. If Rick was guilty, he should be punished. Danny felt strongly about that. But if he wasn't guilty, he shouldn't be held in jail.

Danny sat down heavily on the side of the bed and stared at the floor. He was still sitting there when John came in shortly before noon.

"And what is it this time that's got you about ready to freak out?" John wanted to know. "Would you like to tell Uncle John all about it?"

Danny ignored his feeble attempt at humor. Most of the time he liked his roommate's ready wit, but there were occasions when it bugged him. This was one of those times.

"I just came from the police station," Danny said. "They've got Rick Henderson."

"I've been afraid something like that would happen. With the problems he's got at home, you can hardly expect anything else."

"I guess that's right. But the trouble is, I'm not sure he's guilty and I don't know why."

"I can understand that, too," John went on.

"It isn't because I like the little guy, either," Danny retorted quickly. "I just don't think he's guilty this time, that's all." He paused to breathe deeply. "And I don't know for sure why. That's what gets me so much."

John was quiet for a time. "You said this happened during the basketball game Friday night, didn't you?" he asked suddenly.

"That's right. Why?"

"Did you stop and think where Rick was during Friday night's basketball game? He was with you until after the game, at least!"

Danny's eyes widened incredulously. "That's right! He couldn't have been guilty! He was with me at the time those boys were caught!"

John took Danny into Cedarton to the police station where he talked at length with the chief. After a consultation with the city and county attorneys, the boy was released with their apologies.

"You have no idea how glad we are that you came forward and told us where Rick was on Friday night, Orlis," the city attorney said. "We tried to find out if he was with anyone who could say he was somewhere else during the time of the thefts, but I think he was so frightened he couldn't even think. As far as he was concerned, he was already at the reform school and would have to stay there for a couple of years."

Rick cried when Danny and John took him from the police station.

"Do–do I have to come back and have a trial?" he wanted to know. "Can they still send me to the reform school?"

"Not this time," Danny said. "They know now that you're not guilty."

Rick grinned his relief. "It's great to have a friend like you, Danny. If it hadn't been for you, I'd be locked up right now. If it weren't for you, I'd probably be guilty, too."

"What do you mean by that?"

The boy hesitated before speaking. "Y'know, Billy Wentworth wanted me to go with Tod and Clark and him last Friday night. I might've done it, too, because I was feeling awful low that night. But when you said I could come over and see you, that's what I did instead."

Not until later when he thought of it did Danny think how wonderful it was that God had given him the opportunity to be with Rick and help him. Now he was thinking of something else that the boy had said.

"Billy Wentworth?" he echoed. "And just what did Billy have to do with it?"

Rick's cheeks colored a deep, spreading crimson. "I–I didn't mean to say anything about Bill," he blurted. "I didn't mean to say anything at all about him. I just got to talking, that's all. Skip it."

Danny said no more to Rick about the thefts or who took part in them. He didn't have to. He knew now that Bill Wentworth had been in on it, too. He probably was the leader of the gang. He had that type of personality. And he was clever enough to be able to get away from the police, too, if he had half a chance.

Danny debated whether to go to the authorities with what he knew, but only for a moment. It wasn't fair to Billy to let him get away with something like this. He had to be exposed so he would know that he couldn't get away with anything illegal. He went back to the police station and told them what he had learned.

The chief of police went out to the school to get Billy and bring him back to the station for questioning. At first he would tell them nothing at all.

"I didn't have a thing to do with it," he said arrogantly. "If you want to get the guilty guy, go and get Rick Henderson. He's the one who did it."

"We've talked with him, but he's got an unshakeable alibi," they told him. "One of the Cedarton Bible Institute guys was with him Friday night and he says that Rick was with him in his dormitory room all evening. They went out and had a dish of ice cream a little before ten o'clock and had to wait quite a while to be served because so many basketball fans crowded in for something to eat after the game."

For the first time Billy's face was sallow and sweat moistened his cheeks.

"I– I–" He licked his lips.

"Before we talk with you any longer," the chief said, "I think we had better call your parents."

At first when Billy confessed to what he had done, Mrs. Wentworth refused to believe it.

"You're just saying that, William. You don't really mean it. You're just saying that to hurt Daddy and me."

The boy did not reply, but the answer to what she said was written indelibly in his eyes.

"You wouldn't steal anything." She whirled to face the police chief. "Why would Billy steal?" she wanted to know. "He's always had everything he's wanted. He wouldn't have any reason to steal."

"I don't know why he would do it, Mrs. Wentworth," he answered, his irritation showing. "It's not my place to know the reason. All I'm concerned about, as far as my job is concerned, is doing my duty."

"You aren't going to make him stay in jail, are you?" she demanded, her tears drying suddenly. "You wouldn't do that to *my* son."

"That, of course, is up to the judge," he replied.

Mrs. Wentworth and her husband went to see the judge and got permission for their son to be released to them. Then they went to an attorney to get help in keeping Billy out of the boys' reform school. It was not until the day before the Stockade meeting that she called Danny and asked if she could talk with him.

He paused uncertainly, wondering if she had found out about his visit with the police chief. He would have liked to turn her down, but he had no logical reason for doing that. After all, Billy was one of his Stockaders – or at least he had been. Danny knew that he was supposed to be as interested in Billy as in Rick or any of the rest of the guys.

Mrs. Wentworth came to see him that afternoon. She called him into one corner of the lounge and they sat down, heads close together.

"I find it difficult to come to you this way," she began, her voice trembling. Her hands were twisting nervously at her handkerchief. "But I–I have to talk with you."

This time there was no arrogance or anger in her manner.

"Sure."

"I want to apologize to you for being so difficult about wanting Rick Henderson out of Stockade. It was unchristian of me to be so narrow and unthinking. I see now that Rick needs Brigade as much as Billy does."

"I'm sure he does," Danny replied.

"I have no right to ask this after I was so self-righteous and opinionated regarding Rick, but I've been wondering if you'll take him back in Brigade?"

Danny couldn't help staring at her. "You want him in Stockade?" he asked incredulously.

Desperation lurked in her eyes. "We've got to get him under the influence of the gospel as much as we can if we're going to see him become an upstanding Christian of the sort we want him to be when he's an adult."

"We're anxious to have him in Brigade," Danny told her.

Mrs. Wentworth inhaled thoughtfully. There was still something that bothered her. "But, what about the parents of the other boys?" she wanted to know. "What are they going to think when they find out that Billy is in Brigade, after what he's done?"

Danny could not avoid comparing her situation with that of Rick Henderson. "We didn't let you influence us regarding Rick," he told her, "and we won't let any other parents influence us regarding Billy unless he should become unmanageable or unless we all become convinced that he is apt to lead some of the other guys astray and that Brigade is contributing to it. But I can't conceive of that happening."

Gratitude was in her smile. "Thank you, Danny," she said. "Oh, thank you." She arose to leave. "And thank you so much for not allowing me to talk you into making Rick Henderson stay away from Stockade."

He went to the door with her, they bowed their heads for a moment of prayer, and Mrs. Wentworth was gone. Danny went slowly back to his room. This was something he had never imagined would happen. Mrs. Wentworth had actually thanked him for standing firm. It made him realize again that God often worked in strange ways and ways that were hard to understand.

* * *

Kay was still going out with Walt Sherman occasionally. It was quite obvious that she enjoyed his company, and he was quick to tell his friends how much he enjoyed dating Kay. According to the gossip around CBI, they were together.

Danny was one of the first to hear it, of course. And, as usual, he pretended not to be upset about it. But that was only a sham, an act for the other kids at school. Actually, the hurt was deep and only the approach of Christmas made staying at school tolerable.

It was only three weeks until the Christmas holidays and he could go back to the Angle – at least for a while. He didn't think he had ever looked forward to going back home with such eagerness. He would be away from the school and Kay and Walt and everything else that reminded him that he wasn't with her anymore. Being at home for a while might make it possible for him to start forgetting. He hadn't been very successful in forgetting her yet.

Danny had just about decided not to come back to Cedarton Bible Institute the second semester. He had to get away from Kay and have time to think.

It was then that he got a letter from his mother. She wrote that she had just gotten word from Mrs. Milburn that Kay could come and spend Christmas at the Angle.

Danny gasped. That couldn't be true! It had to be some sort of an ugly joke. But there it was in his mother's firm handwriting.

I thought Kay would be so lonely at
Christmas time that I wrote Mrs. Milburn

and asked her if she would write the school and tell them it is all right for her to spend the holidays with us. It won't be like being home, but it will be better than staying in Cedarton over the vacation period.

Love, Mom

CHAPTER 9

COMPANY FOR CHRISTMAS

Danny stared at the letter in his hand as though he could not quite comprehend it. He could understand why his parents had asked Kay to spend the Christmas holiday at the Angle. Going back to Mexico where her mother lived was so far it would cost a great deal to make the trip, more than a widowed missionary would be able to spare. And, as his mother wrote, staying at school was no way to spend the Christmas holidays, that was sure.

At first it was disconcerting for him to have his parents write and invite Kay in spite of the fact that he would be so uncomfortable. Then he realized that they couldn't have known that he was no longer with Kay or that she was dating Walt Sherman.

He read the letter over again before putting it up on his dresser. The chances were that Kay would be as embarrassed about going up to the Angle for Christmas with him being there as he would be at having her there. She would probably go home with one of her girl friends for Christmas.

Or so he told himself.

John agreed with that deduction, but with a disconcerting twist.

"I've seen Kay with Peggy Sherman a lot lately," he began.

Danny nodded. He had seen her with Walt's sister, too. And even that had bothered him.

"I've got a hunch she's going to ask Kay to go home with her for Christmas."

Danny winced and found something to do so he could discontinue the conversation. He didn't even want to think about that possibility. Even then, it kept him awake that night.

The following afternoon Kay sought out Danny in the corridor in front of the school post office.

"If you have the time, Danny," she said, "I'd like to talk with you for a minute or two."

"Sure thing. Let's go down to the snack shop and have some coffee or a cup of tea."

They went to the basement lunchroom and ordered.

"I suppose you know what I want to talk with you about," she said after a time.

"Mom's letter?" he asked.

She nodded.

"I was so surprised when I heard from her. I didn't expect to get an invitation to go up to your place for the holidays this year."

His scowl deepened and he was afraid that the color was creeping up into his cheeks.

"I thought you would be going home with Peggy and Walt," he told her irritably.

"I could." Her cheeks were flushed. "I have an invitation to spend Christmas with them."

"Then why don't you do it?"

She laid a hand on his arm appealingly. "Danny," she said softly, "please don't be like that. Don't make this any harder than it is."

His gaze met hers.

"I'm sorry," he answered. "Truly I am, but I can't help being a little resentful." There was a moment's silence. "What did you want to talk with me about, Kay?"

"Are you sure you want to know?"

"Of course I do. I've told you that I'm sorry for that crack."

"Well, I got this letter from your mother asking me to come up to the Angle for Christmas. I didn't want to accept before I talked with you about it, but I guess I already have my answer."

"What do you mean by that?" His eyes softened. "Were you thinking about coming?"

She hesitated.

"I really don't have any other place to go where I would feel free to go," she said. "And I have been wondering whether I should accept your parents' invitation or not. I wouldn't want to do it and embarrass you, Danny."

He was about to ask her how she thought he could help being embarrassed and upset in having her come to his home and spend the Christmas holidays after what had happened. But he couldn't do that. He thought too much of her to have her lonely at Christmas time just because he might find it uncomfortable to have her around.

"I'd like very much to have you come, Kay," he said with a suddenness that surprised both of them.

"You would?"

"You should know that by this time. You've always been someone special to all of us – to our whole family."

Her smile faded. "Danny, I want you to answer me honestly. Will you be embarrassed if I come?"

He paused for a moment. "I'll level with you, Kay. It's going to make me uneasy having you in the house and knowing that you and I aren't going to be dating anymore."

"I was afraid of that."

"I haven't finished yet. But I would love to have you, and I know that Mom and Dad and the twins will, too. So I hope you'll come."

That settled the matter as far as Kay was concerned. She thanked him and asked when they would be leaving and if there was going to be anyone else at the house over the holidays so she would know whether to bring any extra gifts.

Danny enjoyed talking with Kay that afternoon.

It was the first time they had said more than a few words to each other since they broke up. However, it was disturbing too. He couldn't understand why he had insisted that Kay spend the Christmas holidays at the Angle. It was bad enough knowing that he wasn't going to be dating her anymore. Now she was going to be right at the house where they would be together for several days. He wouldn't have any opportunity to avoid her. That was going to make him feel worse than he did already. He closed his eyes, but he was unable to sleep until well after midnight. And when he woke up in the morning he was as disturbed as before. Only it was too late. He couldn't change things then.

The following night Tod and Clark didn't come to Brigade, but Billy Wentworth was there. He came in uneasily, standing just inside the door for a time as though he was afraid someone would tell him that he had to leave.

"Hi, Bill." Danny went over to him quickly, smiling a welcome. "I'm sure glad you came."

The boy relaxed a bit. "Mom said it was all right for me to come tonight. She said that she'd talked to you and you said it would be OK."

"Of course it's all right for you to come. We're all glad that you're here."

Billy winced. "After what happened?"

"Neither one of us can go back and undo what happened, Billy, but we can go on from here and see that it doesn't happen again."

The boy nodded gratefully.

Someone else came up just then and Danny didn't get a chance to talk with Billy Wentworth about his need for making a personal commitment of his life to the Lord Jesus Christ. But that chance would come. He was sure of that now. And when it did, he felt that Billy would see that walking with Christ was the only way to live a happy, satisfying life.

Before the meeting started Rick Henderson came up to him. "I was going to call you this afternoon, Danny," he said, "but Mom said I should wait until tonight. She said you'd get so tired of having me bother you that you'd never want me to call again."

"I doubt that," Danny said, rumpling the boy's hair. "But, what's on your mind?"

"I've just been wondering something. Are we going to have Brigade over the holidays?"

Danny read the disappointment in the boy's eyes. "I'm sorry, Rick," he said, "but I'm not going to be in Cedarton until school starts again after New Year's, so we won't be having our meetings."

"Oh." Rick's regret was sharp. "I was just wondering."

Something about his manner disturbed Danny enough to cause him to ask about it. "What's troubling you?"

"Nothing." Rick shrugged and would have turned away but Danny grasped him by the shoulder.

"Now, wait a minute, Rick. What is it about my

not going to be around during Christmas that bothers you so much?"

"There's no reason, I guess." The boy was fighting to keep the tears away, "except that I've got to stay with the neighbor lady."

Danny could scarcely believe it. "You mean your mother's not going to be home?"

Rick swallowed hard. Once he had started to talk to Danny he had to continue. "She told me last night that she's made arrangements for me to stay with the people across the street. And that's sure not going to be much of a Christmas."

Danny's forehead wrinkled. He couldn't understand how a mother could leave her son at Christmas time. Impulsively he bent down. "Rick, does your mother work anywhere?"

"Sure. She's a waitress at that truck stop on the edge of town." His eyes narrowed questioningly. "Why?"

"Would she be home now?"

"Not tonight. She's working. She let me off here at the church on the way to the cafe."

Danny said no more to him about it, but a plan was forming in his mind. He couldn't say that he was exactly ecstatic about spending Christmas with Rick Henderson, but he couldn't have that boy spending Christmas with a neighbor when there was room for him at home and Danny knew that his parents would have room for him and would be glad to have him.

As soon as the meeting was over that night, Danny

went out to the cafe where the boy's mother worked. He recognized her immediately, even before she came to wait on him. She was as slight and harried as her son, with too much makeup and the same haunting look in her eyes. She came over to Danny wearily.

"What you goin' to have?" she asked, shoving a greasy menu in front of him. "Or do you want to take a look at this?"

"No, thank you. I really came in to talk to you if you could spare a minute or two."

She stiffened. "Now listen, buster, I've got me a boyfriend. I ain't got time for the likes of you, even if I wasn't almost old enough to be your mother."

"I'm Danny Orlis," he said quietly.

Her eyes widened. "Are you the guy Rick's been talking about all the time?"

"I'm his Brigade leader if that's what you mean. And he has called me several times and has come out to the school to see me a few times."

She looked around to be sure she didn't have any customers and sat down across from Danny.

"I just remembered I ain't thanked you yet for what you done for Rick when the cops accused him of stealin' stuff out of cars. If it hadn't been for you, he'd have been in that reform school for sure."

"I just told the authorities the truth," Danny reminded her. "And as soon as they found out that he wasn't guilty they were anxious to release him."

"I know, but if you hadn't let him come out to see

you, he wouldn't have had no proof that he wasn't guilty." The color came up into her cheeks. "I do want to thank you for helping Rick then and–and all those other times."

"That's all right," Danny said uncomfortably. "I'm glad to be able to do what I can."

"He doesn't have it so easy," she went on. "I work a lot and, you see, I've got this boyfriend who doesn't exactly like Rick and–" she shrugged expressively.

"Rick tells me that you're going to be gone over the Christmas holidays."

Mrs. Henderson's cheeks flushed.

"I suppose you think I'm a rotten mother runnin' away from him at a time like Christmas, but I ain't had no vacation all year and the cafe is closed, so I–uh–figured I'd go away for a few days. A girl friend and me are going to Chicago to see a few shows and get some new clothes and–and–" Her voice trailed away.

"What do you plan on doing with Rick?" he asked.

"I've already taken care of that. A neighbor across the street is going to keep him. He don't like the idea much, but it's the best I can do."

When Danny suggested that he take Rick home with him over Christmas, she eyed him suspiciously.

"He might like it better being with you, but I can't pay no more than twenty-five dollars for the week. I ain't got much money and–"

"This isn't going to cost you anything. If I can

take him with me, I'll see that he gets up to the Angle where we live and back to Cedarton in time for school after New Year's."

She stared at him. This couldn't be true. There had to be something wrong. "You mean that you'll take my kid for a whole week for free?"

"That's right."

She shook her head disbelievingly. "You know, I can understand why Rick thinks so much of you. You're somethin' else!"

Danny supposed that was meant to be a compliment, but he wasn't sure.

CHAPTER 10

BAD TEMPER AND SERIOUS CONSEQUENCES

Danny made arrangements for Kay and Rick and himself to ride up to Warroad with one of the guys from there who went to CBI. A friend of the Orlis family took them up to the Angle, driving on the winter road through the muskeg. Danny was glad to have Rick along. The boy talked incessantly.

"Have you still got your crow, Blackie?" he asked, his voice alive and quivering with excitement. "And what about Laddie? Is he still around?"

Danny had forgotten he told Rick about his pets. "I've still got Laddie," he said, "although he's getting quite old by now and he doesn't do much except sleep by the fire. But Blackie's long gone. He flew away one year and never came back. I don't know whether he got tired of us or if an owl or a hunter got him."

Wonder widened Rick's eyes. "I'd sure like to

catch me a crow so I could teach him to talk. Do you suppose we could do that while we're here, Danny?"

Danny grinned. "I'm afraid we aren't going to find any crows around the Angle this time of year. They headed south months ago."

The boy was disappointed. "If I catch me a crow next summer, will you help me teach him to talk, Danny? Will you?"

He laughed. "You'd better get the crow first. That's not quite as easy as it sounds."

Rick was silent for a moment and Danny glanced at Kay who was sitting in the front seat. She was prettier and more desirable than he had ever known her to be. For a long minute the ache in his heart grew. He hadn't realized how much he really thought of her until now that they no longer were together.

Maybe, he reasoned hopefully, this trip would help him to get things straightened out with her. They were going to be at the Angle for more than a week. There would be plenty of time for them to talk.

That night before going to bed Danny knelt for a long while on the cold wooden floor and talked with God about Kay and the problem that had come up between them. "Dear God," he prayed quietly, "help me to be able to talk with her and to make her see that we should be together. Help me to make her understand that we can serve You here on the Angle just as effectively as we can anywhere else."

Rick was excited about everything at the Orlis

home. He wanted to be outside constantly and he wanted Danny to be with him. Danny did get tired of constantly doing the things Rick wanted to do, but in another way, it was good to have him there. He kept him so busy there was no opportunity for Carl and Mary Orlis and the twins to notice that there was anything amiss between him and Kay. He would have to tell them sometime, he knew, but he didn't feel up to it right then. He could write to them when he got back to CBI if they didn't see that something was wrong and ask about it.

Christmas day came and went. Danny had bought a couple of inexpensive gifts for Rick and a book of poetry for Kay in addition to the gifts he got for his own family. Rick's face clouded as he opened the packages.

"You know, Danny," he said, his lips trembling, "I didn't think to get you nothin', and here you got me *two* presents!"

"I just wanted to get you a little something to help you remember your trip up here," Danny told him.

"Remember it?" The boy's voice was tinged with awe. "I've never had such a wonderful trip in my whole life! I'll never forget comin' up here! Never!"

"I feel the same way," Kay broke in. "This is almost as good as being home with Mom. In fact, this is almost like home to me."

For the rest of the evening it was difficult for Danny to realize that there was anything wrong between him and Kay. She laughed and joked the way she always did and talked with him the same as she had before there was any difficulty between them.

He was beginning to think that perhaps the trip had already accomplished what he had been praying it would and that their problems were being ironed out. He began to think that by the time they went back to CBI they would be together the same as before. However, the day before they were to return to Cedarton, he learned that nothing had changed. Kay was still as determined as ever not to go out with him.

"I'm sorry, Danny," she told him as they walked together along the snow-covered path from the Orlis home to the neighbors across the way. "I know you find it hard to understand, but there's really no use in our going over this anymore. We've already talked it out. I understand your position and I think you understand mine. The way things are I don't feel that we should be going out together."

His temper flamed. "Do you think that's fair to me, Kay?" he demanded. "And is it fair to yourself?"

She paused and faced him.

"I'm convinced that it's God's way, Danny," she replied. "And if it is His will, then it's best for us, whether it seems hard or not."

He shook his head incredulously.

"I can't understand you. If I didn't know you better I'd swear that you were just using this as an excuse, and that the real reason would be because you were dating Walt and found what you like in him so much more than you like me."

"That's not it at all," she protested. "Walt and I go out together because we enjoy each other's company. Nothing more."

"But you won't go out with me for the same reason."

"It wasn't the same, Danny," she said, struggling to find the words to explain herself. "But, please, Danny, let's not spoil our last day here at the Angle by talking about that."

His temper exploded.

"You're the one I can't figure out! Nothing you say makes sense. You refuse to go out with me, even on a friendly basis. Then you ask me not to do anything to spoil our last day here. I think you'd better get things straight, Kay."

"I'm sorry, Danny," she said, close to tears. "Really, I am."

Then before he could say more she turned and went back to the house. Danny watched her until she reached the back door, took off her boots and went inside. Then he whirled and strode angrily away.

He should have known better than to have told Kay that it was all right for her to spend the Christmas holidays at the Angle. They were as far apart as ever. If anything, her being there had made things worse. She was still as determined as ever not to date him. He supposed the next thing she would tell him was that she and Walt were engaged. But she wouldn't want to hurt him by it. He didn't know what she expected. After all, he was human. He wasn't made of brass.

Danny was still thinking about Kay and the difficult situation in which they found themselves when he heard a young voice calling out behind him.

"Danny! Danny! Wait up!"

He paused and turned slowly. If there was ever a time when he hadn't wanted to see Rick Henderson, this was it!

"Where are you going?"

Danny glared at the boy. "What's with you?" he demanded coldly.

Rick's expression changed incredulously. "I was just wondering if I could go with you?"

Danny scowled at him. "No, you can't go with me! I don't know what's gotten into you the last few days, Rick. I'd like to turn around just once without having *you* there wanting to go with me!"

Surprise gleamed in the boy's eyes. He started to speak, lips trembling, but the words would not come.

Danny saw how he had hurt the boy, but in his anger he didn't care.

"Go on back to the house, will you? I want to be alone for a little while!" With that he turned deliberately and strode away.

Danny Orlis didn't know when his mind had been in such a turmoil as it was now. Again he was tempted to pretend to be as interested in missions as Kay was. He loved her enough even to go out on the mission field if that was what it would take to get her. But he couldn't bring himself to that deceit. He had to weigh the matter carefully, to go over it in his mind until he knew for certain that his decision was right.

At times he felt that God did want him on the mission field and that he was violating his commitment to Christ when he planned for any other future. On the other hand, his love for the bush country of the north was strong. If he became a missionary to some distant place he would have to give up the Angle. He wouldn't be able to be close enough to get home. He wouldn't be able to walk the snow-covered paths that had meant so much to him as a kid. He wouldn't be able to draw a bead on a moose or a deer or to fish for walleyes or northerns in the cold water. He wouldn't be able to see the sunsets that still took his breath away.

Would God have given him such a love for the north if He was going to lead him to the far places? This he still battled without answer.

How long Danny was gone he did not know. However, the sun was almost down and the shadows were stretching long and dark across the new white snow. Reluctantly he turned at last and headed back to the house. When he got there his mother met him at the door.

"Oh, there you are, Danny. You were gone for so long I was beginning to get concerned about you."

"I just went for a walk," he said cryptically, hoping he wouldn't have to make any further explanation.

"Has Rick been with you?"

"Rick?" He glanced about, quickly. "He came out where I was some time ago, but he left. Didn't he come back to the house?"

"We haven't seen him for an hour or so."

Danny shivered convulsively. "He came out and talked with me for a couple of minutes," Danny said lamely, "but when he left I thought he was coming straight back to the house."

"I met him as I was coming in," Kay said. "He told me that he was going out for a walk with you."

Danny's cheeks flushed and his mouth went dry and coppery. Kay was eying him curiously. She must know that Rick had found him and that he had gotten angry with the boy for no reason at all and had sent him away.

"Did you look in his room?" he asked. "Maybe he went in to lie down or read something?"

"Oh, no," his mother said quickly. "I know that he isn't in the house. I've looked every place."

Fear wiped away the last traces of Danny's anger. Rick thought so much of him that he wanted to be with him every minute he could. And what had he done? He'd lost his temper and told him to leave him alone! There was no knowing where the boy had gone. And it was Danny's fault! Whatever happened, he was the cause of it!

CHAPTER 11

THE SEARCH

On any other occasion Danny would have been quick to act. This time, however, he was helpless for the moment, stunned by what had happened and his own part in causing it. He looked to his dad for guidance.

"What do you think we should do?" he asked. "Get all the neighbors to come and look for him?"

Carl hesitated, staring out across the bleak, icy scene. They would have to act promptly and in the right way if they wanted to keep the matter from getting any worse.

"I'll have Ron take the snowmobile and get all the men he can," Carl said. "But in the meantime, I think we ought to go out and look for Rick. It'll take some time to get help here, and I'm sure he's going to be mighty cold, even now."

Danny nodded. No one had to tell him what his

dad meant. It was already twenty-four degrees below zero. It was one of those deceptive winter days that seemed much warmer than it actually was. Since there was no wind blowing the weather didn't seem to be so cold, until one was out in it for a while. Then it would bite through all but the heaviest of clothing and gnaw its way into the marrow of the bones.

And the temperature would probably drop another five or ten degrees after the sun had set. Rick was dressed warmly, but not warmly enough to be out for a prolonged period in such cold. Danny was sure that Rick couldn't make it through the night knowing as little as he did about the woods.

"I'll go back to the place where he came to me," he said aloud, "and see if I can trail him in the snow."

"That's a good idea," his dad replied. "And we'd better get with it. It isn't going to be too long until sunset."

Danny turned abruptly and made his way up the trail. Moments later he heard the snowmobile start and saw Ron racing along the frozen creek in the direction of the Olsen cabin, their nearest neighbor.

They had to get help, he realized, but there wasn't time for anyone to get over to the Orlis place to get a search party organized and looking for Rick before dark. The men would come prepared with powerful flashlights and would look through the long, bitter night, of course, but anyone who knew anything about the north knew how hopeless it would be to try to find Rick after darkness closed in. He could be three feet beyond the beam of the flashlight, and they could go right by, unless he was able to cry out to them.

A terrible dread took hold of Danny. What had happened was his fault and his alone. He should have let Rick go with him. He knew that now. Actually, he knew what he should have done when he saw the hurt in the boy's eyes and realized that he had been the cause of it. But he had let his anger engulf any compassion he had for Rick. And now this had happened.

He strode on miserably, not realizing that he was almost running.

It was as though the events of that afternoon had suddenly loosed the blinders from his eyes so he could see himself as he really was. He had lost his temper and exploded to both Kay and Rick. For the first time he realized that he was out of the will of God. Had he been following the Lord's leading he would have approached the discussion with Kay as calmly as she did, and when Rick came along, he would have been kind and gentle to him.

Back at CBI the year before he had made a decision to consecrate his life and allow Him to lead him wherever He wanted him. He tried to make himself believe that he was following that leading when actually he wanted the reins of his life back in his own control.

He tried to make himself believe that God would have him work among the people he knew on the Angle when actually he loved it there and wanted to find an excuse to live there. Kay had seen the selfishness and self-deceit in his life and was afraid that the same thing might happen to her if she kept going out with him. So she had put God first and he had been furious.

Now this had happened to Rick, whose fault had been that he loved Danny too much. And if the boy wasn't found until it was too late, it would be Danny's fault. No one else would blame him for it. They probably wouldn't even understand if he told them. They would say that Rick had gotten into trouble because he wandered away and got lost, but Danny would know better.

He prayed desperately that God would help them to find Rick before he hurt himself or was frozen to death. He asked God's forgiveness, too, for the way in which he had turned aside from Him to follow his own way.

"Whatever You have for me," he prayed inwardly, "that's what I want. I love it here and I want to stay here. I think You know that. But even more, I want to follow Your leading. I'm willing to go wherever You want me to go and do whatever You want me to do, even if it means that I may never get back to the Angle."

Danny had prayed a similar prayer the spring before, but this one was different. The other came from a stirring of his emotions. He meant it, of course, but he had never counted the cost. He had never before weighed it against all else in life.

Now, however, he did just that. And strangely enough, he didn't even consider Kay as he yielded himself to God's guidance. He didn't think of that decision as a way of getting her back. He thought only of consecrating his life to God and letting Him lead.

At the point on the path where Rick had approached Danny, he stopped and looked about. It wasn't difficult to find the boy's footprints. He had turned and walked a few steps, before turning to look at Danny again.

Danny winced as he realized how Rick must have felt standing there and watching him stride up the trail and out of sight. Rick must not have known just what to do then. His footprints were an uneven distance apart and once or twice he stopped and turned around as though expecting Danny to come back for him.

The boy stayed on the path for some distance before leaving it and angling into the bush. Danny had no difficulty in following him until he reached the snowmobile trail Ron had used. Danny looked in both directions, dismay churning within him. There was no way of knowing whether Rick had gone away from the Orlis place or toward it.

Danny hesitated momentarily, praying for guidance. Then he started down the trail and away from home. He followed it for almost half a mile, studying the soft snow on either side of the snowmobile track carefully for some sign that the boy had gone that way. Although the trail was wide enough for a person to walk on with ease it seemed incredible that the snowmobile would blot out every footprint of Rick's if the boy went that way. When he finally reached the point where the snowmobile left the main trail to turn into the Olsen buildings and there was no sign that Rick had gone that way Danny stopped, reluctantly, and turned back. In a way he doubted that he had ever seen the boy's footprints in the snow at all. But he knew that he had.

Danny glanced up at the darkening sky. The sun was only a dot of fire above the trees and shadows were blending together. It wouldn't be long until night would close in. If Rick wasn't found by that time, he wouldn't be found alive, that was certain.

Whirling, a prayer in his heart, Danny ran up the trail toward home. Two or three hundred yards beyond the place where Rick's footprints approached the snowmobile trail, Danny saw a small footprint. He stopped briefly, heart pounding, and examined it. At first, hope surged within him. Then it died as quickly as it came. Those were Rick's tracks, all right, but they could have been made that morning or the day before. It hadn't snowed for at least that long. Danny prayed again, in desperation.

Another fifty yards up the trail he saw another footprint and another. Danny's excitement grew. Maybe-just maybe-his mother had been mistaken and Rick was somewhere in the house. He remembered when he was about Rick's age that he had pulled a trick like that after his dad punished him. And he had gotten another spanking when they found him in the house after calling out all the neighbors to look for him.

Near the barn Danny saw that the small footprints left the snowmobile trail. He almost missed them and had to go back to make sure. But there they were, heading straight for the barn door. He followed them hurriedly.

"Rick!" he called, peering into the darkness. "Rick! Are you here?"

No answer.

"Rick!" He stepped inside, blinking momentarily as his eyes accustomed themselves to the dim light. "Rick! Are you here?"

For a time the silence was deafening. His own anguish surged. Then he heard a muffled sob coming from the far corner of the small building.

"Rick!" he cried, rushing forward.

There in the corner of the horse stall lay the boy, huddled in the hay against the manger. Danny dropped to his knees beside him.

"Rick! What's wrong?"

The small boy sat up slowly, scrubbing at his eyes. Danny felt a sudden surge of relief and a prayer of thanksgiving welled wordlessly in his heart.

"I–I'm sorry I gave you such a bad time," the boy blurted. "I didn't mean to, Danny. Really and truly I didn't."

"Who told you that you gave me a bad time?" Danny asked.

"I didn't mean to be a nuisance to you. I just wanted to be with you for a while, that's all. You're the only friend I've got." His voice grew taut and he started to cry again.

Danny gathered the lad into his arms. "Just take it easy, Rick. You don't make yourself a nuisance with me, that's for sure."

Rick looked up, confusion marring his gaunt young face. "But you told me that you wanted me to go away and leave you alone! You said that I follow you around all the time!"

Danny nodded. "I know I said that, Rick, and it wasn't very nice of me to say it. I've been sorry about it ever since."

This Rick refused to believe. "You wouldn't have said it if you hadn't meant it," he told him. "You just pretend to love me, Danny, the same as everybody else."

Danny's face was taut.

"I do love you, Rick," he repeated. "And I am sorry I spoke to you the way I did. I don't have any excuse for it. It's just that I had a real personal problem on my mind and I was so upset that I hardly knew what I was saying."

Rick wiped the tears from his eyes. "Is that the honest truth, Danny?"

"It's the honest truth." Danny put his arms about him. "But I'm going to tell you something else that's even more important than that. Did anyone ever tell you that Jesus Christ loves you?"

The boy nodded his head. "You did once, Danny."

"He does," Danny continued. "He loves you more than your mother does, or me, or anyone else in all the world. He loves you so much that He died on the cross to save you."

Rick listened intently as Danny again explained the way of salvation to him. He outlined in simple terms God's plan to save those who called on His name. Using Bible verses, he showed Rick that everyone is a sinner and needs to be saved. Then he went on to show that God knew no one could live up to His laws so He sent the Lord Jesus Christ to earth to live a sinless life, to be nailed to the cross and die and rise again so men could confess their sin and put their trust in Jesus to save them.

He had gone over the same thing in Brigade a number of times using some of the same Bible verses, but Rick must not have been listening. Either that or he didn't understand. This time he grasped it.

"Do you mean that God would save *me?*" he asked doubtfully.

"That's right. All you have to do is to let Him." Still, Rick wasn't so sure. "I couldn't live a Christian life," he said. "I never can do anything right."

"That's just it," Danny continued, "you don't have to. God will help you to live the way you should."

As far as Rick was concerned, that settled it.

Danny knelt with him in the hay and he asked God to take away the sin and give him a new life. Rick was smiling broadly as he went into the house with Danny a few moments later.

That night after the excitement was over and Rick had dinner and had gone to bed Danny turned to Kay.

"Would you go for a little walk with me?" he asked, keeping his voice quiet enough so he wouldn't be overheard.

She hesitated.

"It's all right," he continued. "I just want to talk to you. I'm not going to give you a bad time."

She got her coat and they went out into the still, cold night together.

They walked for a dozen yards or so before Danny spoke.

"I want to ask your forgiveness for the way I talked to you this afternoon," he said. "I had no right to be so angry."

"That's all right."

"No, it isn't all right. It was inexcusable. I want you to know how sorry I am."

"I forgive you, Danny," she said. "And I know how you must feel about all of this. Only–"

"I understand it now, Kay," he continued. "I just want you to know that this afternoon while we were looking for Rick I came to understand some things about myself – some things that I didn't like to admit."

He went on to tell her how he had tried to deceive

himself into thinking that God was leading him to the Angle when actually, he just wanted that for himself. He wanted it so much it drew him away from God's plan for his life.

"I told God that I had finally come to see that I was rebelling against Him and that I want His will for my life, whatever that may be."

Her gaze met his. "Oh, Danny!"

"I don't know for sure if He's going to lead me to the mission field or not," he said, "but as far as I'm concerned, the matter is settled. I'm going to do what He wants me to do."

They spent a long time outside that evening, talking quietly until, at last, the cold drove them in. The rest of the family had gone to bed, but the light was burning in the living room.

"If we'd known everyone had cleared out we could have come in here an hour ago," Danny said, "and been warm."

Kay's gaze met his. "Was it cold out there?"

He grinned. This had been the most wonderful Christmas season he had ever experienced. Rick Henderson was a Christian now and everything was all right between him and Kay again. He hadn't asked her about it. He didn't have to. The answer was written in her eyes.

www.ingramcontent.com/pod-product-compliance
Lightning Source LLC
Chambersburg PA
CBHW070911100726
47907CB00008B/2280